# THE STAIRWELL

Dean Bryant

# CONTENTS

*For Rachel,*
*Without whom, this book, and many other things, would not be possible.*

# <u>PROLOGUE</u>

## BRANDON

I pulled up outside my family home at around 9pm and was surprised to see that there were no lights on in the house. I parked in the driveway and approached the front door, but even before inserting my key into the lock, I knew something was wrong. A feeling of intense trepidation slowly crept into my subconscious and my hands trembling as I struggled to unlock the door to the Victorian mid-terraced house that I had called home for several years. I managed to turn the key in the lock and entered the house to the same sight I saw most afternoons, baby toys strewn across the black sheepskin rug, the once romantic living room in a state of semi chaos. Yet something was different - the house was silent. My mind tried to recall the last time the house was this void of sound, yet it could not. My three-year-old daughter, Lily, always ensured that the small two-bedroom home was constantly alive with the continuous yet reassuring sounds of a child at play. This unexpected silence felt oppressive, and I was terrified, though I didn't know why.

I stepped over the discarded Duplo bricks that on many nights acted as traps in the darkness, waiting to be trodden on, I looked around the room for signs of normality. My unexplained panic grew with each step I took through the sitting room as I waited to be faced with whatever it was that caused my dread. I peered through the doorway into the kitchen, searching for my family. A dark shape passed my peripheral vision, causing me to turn and face it, but when I did, only darkness stared back at me.

Suddenly, the most awful sound I have ever heard echoed down from upstairs. I heard Lily screaming and crying, but not her usual cry of hunger or the need for attention. The sound rooted my body in place, as what felt like tentacles of terror constricted me in their dark embrace. I forced myself into action. My legs – they did not feel like my own – heavy, propelling me towards the staircase. With each step I took, the staircase seemed to grow another step, as though they would not allow me to reach the top. My heartbeat pulsed fear through my veins as thick as molten rock. There was another sound, this time even worse – the sound of complete silence, again.

I eventually reached the top of the stairs, and as I approached our bedroom, an invisible force pushed me to my hands and knees, and as much as I tried I could not stand back up. Crawling now, using all my strength just to move along the corridor, the entire house came alive. The bathroom door swung open, the shower turned on, from downstairs the sound of the TV reached my ears, and all the lights in the house turned on, burning brighter than the energy saving bulbs usually allowed. A rumbling noise then assaulted my brain, seemingly coming from everywhere in the house. It was so deep that I could feel it vibrate even in my bones.

Unable to move my hands from the floor to protect my ears, I tried to scream out my wife's name, but I could not hear my own voice over the rumbling. I edged closer to Lily's bedroom, and finally I could see inside. I saw Stephanie sitting in the rocking chair, with Lily on her lap. Before I could move any closer, the terrible rumble stopped. The only sound that I could now hear was the creaking of wood as Stephanie rocked in the chair, her usual way of getting Lily to sleep. All the lights in the house went back out, except for in the bedroom, and the sound from the TV below ceased. I was now again able to stand and rose back to my feet. I was only feet away from the chair where my wife and baby daughter sat, but the scene seemed so wrong and unnatural, and I heard a deep, guttural sob that must have come from me. Lily was lying across Stephanie's legs, her head dangling at a horrifying angle.

"Steph! What happened?!" I scream at her, tears meandering the contours of my face. There was no reply. In fact, she didn't even acknowledge that I was there, but carried on humming You Are My Sunshine, the gentle tune she used to get Lily to sleep. As I approached her, it struck me that her face was terribly pale, with dark, thick veins stretching out from around her eyes like the roots of an old tree. Her gaze remained stationary, and when I looked into her beautiful, familiar hazel eyes full of kindness were replaced with pure white irises, open, but not seeing. I took Lily from her lap, and when I lifted her into my arms, I knew it was already too late. Her tiny body was limp in my arms, and as I lowered her to the ground to try to breathe life into her infant lungs, the realisation had already hit me that my daughter was dead. Despite knowing the truth, with the palms of my hands, I tried to bring a beat back to her heart.

Still Stephanie continued to rock in the chair and hum the tune over and over. When I finally allowed myself to accept the truth, I cuddled her close against my chest and kissed the top of her head, her soft blonde hair sticking to my tear-stained face. I gently carried her over to her bed and lay her in it. Though I knew she was gone, I could not simply abandon her on the floor. For the first time since the scene in the bedroom, I felt capable of conscious thought. What the hell had happened? Did Stephanie kill Lily? There was no way she was capable of this, was there? What was wrong with her face? I'd never seen anything like it, the pure black veins around her eyes contrasted against the marble like quality of her face, even paler than she normally looks.

In my state of utter despair, I didn't know what to do next. I shouted her name louder and louder and was too afraid to approach her. There was still no sign that she even knew I was with her, and I edged closer and closer to the rocking chair, gingerly gripping her shoulder. My hand made contact with her skin, as she was wearing her vest that she always wears when she didn't expect to leave the house again that evening. As soon as my skin touched hers, it felt as though hundreds of tiny needles pierced my hand. Instinctively, I withdrew and examined it, but there were no visible marks. The contact seemed to make her finally aware that I was there. She stood bolt upright and let out the most awful scream. Her head lolled back as she stared at the ceiling and continued to let out the horrible sound. I tried to shake her, to bring her out of this awful state and back to me, but even contact with her clothes caused the invisible needles to penetrate my skin, the sensation more extreme with every attempt.

Completely helpless, I backed into the corner of the room, my eyes wide with terror, and slumped to the floor, a useless, sobbing wreck. As suddenly as it started, the screaming stopped, and as I looked up at her, she began to rotate on the spot, her feet still. Then she left the ground altogether, and she floated a metre or so above the ground, still slowly spinning around. A deep noise escaped her lips, sounding more like a heavy rock being dragged across the ground than the soft, sweet voice of my wife. The sound repeated over and over until I was finally able to discern a single word amongst the awful cacophony.

"Brandon." The chant came slowly at first, then increasingly quicker. A smile spread across her face, but definitely wasn't my wife's.

It was an evil, wicked expression. I witnessed Stephanie's pale skin stretch at the corners of her mouth. Small tears began to form as her mouth opened impossibly wide in a maniacal grin. I could not bear watching yet could not look away as the skin tore all the way to both ears. I fought to not vomit at the crunching and snapping sounds of Stephanie's jaw dislocating and hanging loose from her skull. Somehow, with her lower jaw visibly separate from the upper, she let out a demonic laugh which rang in my head. Every nerve-ending on my body now felt as though it was being plucked like a guitar string by the hand of fear itself. Now, for the first time, Stephanie looked at me with those white eyes, though it was definitely not her in the driver's seat.

Floating through the room towards me, she repeated my name continuously, her impossibly white eyes staring through my own, peering into my soul, my atheist beliefs torn from me by the creature that wore my wife's skin. As she floated closer, the carpet burned and melted into a black mess underneath her. In my desperation, I pleaded with God for this awful nightmare to end as Stephanie extended her arms, the skin on them the same marble white as her face. She reached for me with broken, disfigured fingers. Her face was now centimetres from mine. Despite her jaw hanging grotesquely, a voice echoed from within her. "This is the beginning, Brandon", it said, before the black veins from around her eyes extended out of her face. The last thing I remember seeing that night was those veins snaking their way to my eyes and piercing them, leaving me in pitch blackness. Before I passed out, I could feel the creature slipping away, but not before whispering, for a final time, "just the beginning".

# CHAPTER ONE

## ALICE

Alice White looked into the mirror and sighed. The minute hand of the ever-disobeyed alarm clock on her pristine makeup table/desk had passed at least 360 degrees since she started getting ready, and she still wasn't happy with how she looked. Honestly, though, she rarely was. If you tried to find a man that didn't find her attractive, however, the hour hand would rotate many more times during the search. Her shoulder-length blonde hair hung in loose curls, her eyes were an almost alarming shade of blue and the pale pink colour of her small lips all complemented each other to create a beauty that wouldn't be out of place on any catwalk. Yet all she saw was a chubby, fat girl staring at her through the mirror, despite the fact that she was only a size eight. Alice was rudely awakened from her thoughts of self-depreciation by the sound of her intercom ringing. Her two best friends, Megan and Charlie, were ready to hit the town for another night of unsuccessful man-hunting and overly-successful drinking. Alice knew where they would be headed - their regular stomping ground of the Anglia Ruskin Student Union in her university city of Cambridge. She picked up the intercom and, just before heading out of the door of her cramped student accommodation, she took one final glance into the mirror that, by now, knew her so well. Giving her best smile at herself in the mirror, she made one final attempt at feeling good about herself before meeting her only friends she'd made since starting university.

The hallways in the building where Alice would be residing nine months out of twelve always gave her the creeps. It was a rarity to find the lighting working as it should, and the imagined danger posed by the cold, narrow concrete staircases was always exacerbated by the darkness that almost seemed to follow her through the hallways. She was sure, when recalling her visit to the student digs before starting her psychology degree, that she didn't feel this way in the hallways. She had been so full of excitement at leaving the small village in Cambridgeshire she had lived all her life, that anywhere compared to there felt exciting and full of promise. She hadn't moved very far, though. Her mother's home was less than thirty miles away (twenty-four to be exact, and Alice liked to be exact), so her mother could come and pick her up should she ever feel the need for some home comforts. All of her friends back in her home village had, she realised after leaving, not really cared very much for her at all. They were mainly male. Girls never seemed very keen on her for some reason, which she had put down to her not being attractive enough.

In reality, however, it was jealousy. Most of the girls in the village weren't the prettiest, and felt that if they hung around Alice, their own male friends would undoubtedly prefer her over themselves. Megan and Charlie, however, were the first girls that she had ever met who had aspirations of a career - a desire and passion to have an identifiable feature stronger than the vocation of the man they were married to. Alice was instantly in awe of these two girls and did her best to please them in an effort to create a friendship. That's why she was going out with them tonight, if she was honest with herself. She had no idea that this would be the night she would meet the man who would change her life forever.

Alice passed through the ground floor lobby of her building and saw her friends outside. She was envious of how beautiful they looked. Megan wore a dress that was practically skintight, as she often did. It allowed full view of her generous curves, which practically spilled out of the front of the dress, whilst seeming that another centimetre or two around her behind would cause the material to give in and split. Charlie, on the other hand, didn't have the curves, but Alice was always jealous of her jet-black, ever straight hair, her dark eyes and pale skin clashing in a beautiful fashion. Her clothes showed about as much skin as Megan's, and Alice was sure that she showed less skin when visiting the university swimming pool.

Opening the front door onto the street, Alice had no idea how they weren't freezing to death, the early November air chilling her before she closed the door. Alice was wearing a pair of tight jeans, paired with a simple white top with frills on the seams of the short sleeves. Most of her outfits were of a similar fashion, simple, unrevealing, but didn't completely mask the terrific body that she had underneath (though of course, Alice didn't know that most men would describe her body this way).

"Ally!" screamed Megan and Charlie in unison. The three met in a group hug, before Megan and Charlie parted from Alice to examine her. Both girls felt a pang of jealousy, not knowing that Alice felt the same way about both of them.

"You both look so gorgeous", sighed Alice.

"Says you!" Megan replied.

"The guys are gonna be all over you, Ally. Why don't you try and enjoy it, for once?" It was true, Alice had never been in the Student Union for more than half an hour without a guy who had had at least enough, sometimes more than enough alcohol to feel brave enough to approach her. She always felt that it was some sort of game for the guys, though. Some sort of dare to pull the ugliest girl they could find. Alice didn't reply, as her friends were already deep in conversation about what to drink first. They were both very smart girls, and they both lived by the mantra 'work hard, play hard'. They weren't afraid of leaving the books behind for a night or two.

It didn't take long for them to reach the Student Union. After showing their student cards to the bouncer on the door, they headed straight for the bar and ordered three glasses of wine. Megan insisted on paying, as she often did. It was widely known that her parents were loaded, so the girls rarely put up much of a fight when she offered to pay. Alice found herself staring at the guy at the other end of the bar, in a manner that she never had before. There was something about him that she couldn't escape from. He was leaning against the bar, a pint of beer gripped between his large hands. He was with his friends, however seemed distant from his group, which Ally felt she mirrored with her friends. His leather jacket was tight against the defined body that she could tell lay beneath, his jeans also leaving little to the imagination.

"Helllloooo? Can you hear me Ally, or are you too busy staring at that yummy guy at the bar?" teased Megan, while adjusting the front of her dress which threatened to reveal a little too much at any moment. Alice's cheeks reddened immediately, and she broke her gaze from him and downed her wine.

"I wasn't staring at him, but he is so good looking it's scary..." Alice sighed.

"Go and talk to him!" said Charlie, already feeling envious at the fact that the gorgeous guy had also been taking a few sneak glances over at Ally when she wasn't looking.

To all of their surprise, most of all to Alice's, the gorgeous guy got up and came over to their group. Alice would always associate the song that had just started playing, at a volume she would describe as being too loud, with this man, which was *The Final Countdown*, by the group Europe. It wasn't her favourite song, and as he sauntered over towards her, smiling, she only heard it in her subconscious, but there it would remain.

"Hi there, I'm Niel," he said confidently and with an intoxicating smile, showing his two rows of perfectly white teeth. He held out his hand and offered it to Alice. Megan and Charlie looked at each other, exchanged open-eyed glances, then looked back at Niel. Alice shyly shook his hand and found it hard to look away from his brown-green eyes. His aftershave that he was wearing increased her arousal, she knew instantly—it was Obsession by Calvin Klein.

"I'm Alice," was all she could manage, her shyness overcoming her.

"Alice, that's a beautiful name. I hope you don't think it's weird me coming over - and I don't wanna sound like a creep or anythin', but I couldn't help it. You're the most gorgeous girl I've ever seen." Despite usually having only negative thoughts about her own appearance, Niel made her feel pretty for the first time in her life. She started to feel tipsy, her cheeks filling with blood and colouring her face a bright red, and a genuine smile spread across her face. She didn't know what to say. Should she return a compliment, and if so, about what? Luckily, Niel spoke before she blurted something out.

"Would you mind dancing with me, Alice?" Niel asked, not breaking eye contact with her. Alice didn't think it possible for her to blush more, but somehow managed it.

"I don't really know how..." Alice replied, while looking down at the floor.

"Come on," Niel said with a smile. "Don't be shy. I'll help you." She looked back to Megan and Charlie, who both nodded encouragement. So Alice and Niel headed to the dance floor and danced through some of Alice's favourite songs. When *Livin' on a Prayer* came on, and Alice told Niel that it was her favourite song, he stopped dancing, pulled her close to him, gently placed a hand on the back of her head, and kissed her. It was a passionate kiss, and Alice thought her knees were going to give out from the pleasure. She'd never had a kiss like it before. He wasn't her first, but the others were now hardly even a distant memory compared to Niel. A small 'wow' escaped her lips, and Niel took that as a good sign. They continued to dance into the small hours of the morning, the small steps that they took in between kisses and embraces caused Alice's shoes to almost come off every time due to the sticky floor caused by numerous spilled drinks. Megan and Charlie left without Alice even noticing.

The cool of the night was in stark contrast to the clammy air of the student union, but refreshing, and Alice felt as though she instantly sobered up (she had only had three drinks - or was it four? But she was a known lightweight), which she was happy for. She didn't want to ruin what had been the best night of her life by saying or doing something stupid now. Niel was beside her, his hand warm against hers, the smell of his aftershave still causing her to have small tingles down there whenever she caught wind of it. She'd never taken a guy back to her own place before. Truthfully, she'd never done more than kiss a guy, so she was already heading to new, nerve-wracking territory. So many worries went through her head before coming back around, as if her mind was running an anxiety Ferris wheel. Was her room a mess? Did she shave her legs? What if he didn't like her body? It seemed that Niel could anticipate her concerns, as he brought her out of her angst trance like state.

"Are you sure you're happy with me coming to your place? We can do this another night, if you'd prefer." The sincerity of his offer and the perfect gentlemanly behaviour only made Alice want him more.

When they arrived at Alice's home, her usual feelings towards the corridors and stairwells all but forgotten, they sat on her single bed, on which springs poked towards the surface like the discs of the spine of a skinny child, side by side, and kissed again with increasing passion. They allowed themselves to fall back onto the bed, still embracing one another. Niel cupped her ample breast through her clothing, and to her surprise, Alice made no attempt to stop him. Before she knew it, his other hand was undoing her jeans and going places no man's hand had gone before. Shortly afterwards, she experienced the first orgasm she'd ever had, and at first, she wasn't sure whether she liked it or not. That soon changed, and she couldn't help but gasp and moan while Niel's fingers worked their magic. She hadn't even removed any clothing before Niel gave her another.

After Alice had calmed down, and after lots of kissing, this time using their tongues, Niel undressed himself, and for the first time in her life, her eyes soaked up all the intriguing, sexy areas of his body, his biceps with veins pushing against the surface of his skin, the outlines of his abs shining with a thin layer of sweat. She also couldn't help but notice that he was rock hard, but she was afraid to touch it. Luckily for her, Niel seemed to be much more experienced than her and took the lead throughout. Over the next hour and a half, Alice and Niel made love for the first time, and then the second time.

"Wow," was again all Alice could manage.

"I'll take that as a good sign," Niel said, winking at her with a huge smile on his face. They were both lying naked, without covers, Alice resting her head on Niel's chest.

"That was *incredible*," Alice said with a contented sigh.

"Well, I've gotta go now," Niel said. "See you around". Alice's heart dropped. She never wanted to be the subject of a one-night stand. The idea of being used for sex disgusted her. Niel grinned and said, "I'm joking, of course! Not going anywhere. I'd love it if you would let me stay the night." Alice's face brightened immediately, and she told him that, of course, he can stay. This man was unlike any other, she thought, whilst enjoying the electric touch of each other's naked skin. They kissed, long and passionately, the intensity of it causing Alice's body to be covered in goose bumps. She couldn't have known that the happiness wouldn't last forever.

# CHAPTER TWO

## BRANDON

I must have somehow fallen asleep, as the next thing I knew I woke up sitting in the corner of Lily's room, my arms crossed over my knees, my head resting on my arms. My neck ached like never before, and I felt as though my brain was spinning inside my head. I suddenly remembered everything that had happened the night before. My grief instantly refreshed, and I collapsed flat on the carpet and sobbed for my dead daughter, who was one of only two things in my life that I was proud of, and that I loved. I looked around the room. Her body was nowhere to be seen. Nor was my wife, who was the second recipient of my love. In fact, the room looked entirely normal. The carpet wasn't burned, the rocking chair was back in the corner of the room where it belonged. I started to question myself - had any of this actually happened? Then I became aware of the pain in my hand from when I tried to touch Stephanie. I remembered the feeling of being pricked by hundreds of needles, though there was no sign of injury on my hand.

It definitely happened, I convinced myself, and broke down into sobbing once more. I was crying so hard that I could barely breathe, only short, gasping bursts, sounding like a dying animal. It was now morning, and all of the events from the previous night were running through my mind. What the hell had happened to Stephanie? I'm not a religious person - too much has happened in my life to disprove any idea of a loving higher power, but the only explanation that I can reach is that Stephanie was possessed. Why else would she do what she did? What was wrong with her eyes, and why did it hurt so much when I tried to touch her?

I had no idea what to do next. I tried to call Stephanie, but it went straight to voicemail, which was very unusual for her. She never turned her phone off. I decided to leave a message.

*"Hello Brandon, leave a message if you like, but I don't think Stephanie will be getting it!"* rasped the deep voice on the voicemail message. The receiver fell out of my hand. It was the same voice that Stephanie had spoken to me in last night. In my state of despair, I didn't know what else to do. Would the police believe me? Of course not, I still barely believe it myself. But I could report Stephanie and Lily missing. At least they might find where they are. I'll just have to not tell them everything else. I picked my phone back up and realised that it was still connected to Stephanie's phone, leaving her a long voicemail. I ended the call and dialled two 9s. I hesitated on the third, but dialled it and waited a few seconds until the phone was answered.

"999. What is your emergency?"

"Uhh, it's my wife and daughter." My voice broke on *daughter*, the reality of the situation hitting me again. "They're missing."

"What's your name, sir?" the voice at the other end of the line asked calmly.

"Brandon. Brandon Chapman."

"OK, Brandon, when did you last see your wife and daughter?" I could hear the sympathy in her voice. It was refreshing after the horror of listening to Stephanie's voicemail. I decided to tell her that the last time I had seen them was yesterday afternoon, before I left the house.

"I see, sir. I understand your concern, however, this sort of thing happens from time to time, and it's probably nothing to worry about. Can I please take their names, though?"

"Stephanie and Lily Chapman."

"Thank you, sir. We'll see what we can do. If they do turn up safe and sound, then please call again, and use this reference number." She started giving me the number before I was ready, so I found a pen as quickly as I could. I found one of Lily's crayons and a scrap of paper. I took the number, thanked the operator, then ended the call.

I headed down the stairs, each step a tremendous effort. There were no signs that anything had happened. There were a couple of letters by the front door at the bottom of the stairs. The sitting room was still in the state that I remember seeing it last night, right down to the Duplo block that I had narrowly avoided the night before. I looked around the room, and after not being able to find anything different, I walked into the kitchen. Everything was as it had been the day before here, too; the sink containing the washing up I hadn't done before from lunch the day before, and Lily's beaker still sat on her high chair table, the Peppa Pig one that she loved so much. I sat at the table and pulled my phone back out of my pocket. I tried Stephanie's number again. Straight to voicemail.

*"Hello Brandon. Stephanie isn't available right now. But Lily would like to say hello."* Then the connection dropped, and the call ended. Before a fresh wave of grief had time to wash over me, I heard the familiar sound of a key entering the Yale lock on the front door. The door opened, and Stephanie walked through.

"Brandon! What are you doing here?" Stephanie asked in shock.

"What happened to you?!" Was this real? Was this actually my wife, or was it the same thing I encountered last night?

"What do you mean, what happened to me? I'm fine. What's wrong with you? You look terrible," Stephanie said, looking me up and down. I walked over to her, fearing her, timidly. She set down her bag and reached out to embrace me. Remembering the feeling I had when I last touched her, I flinched and stepped away from her.

"Baby, what's wrong? Cuddle me." I must've looked like a rabbit in headlights as she approached me again and wrapped her arms around me. She smelled different to how she normally does, but other than that, nothing. No needles piercing my body, no demonic voice. Her eyes were normal. What was going on? Surely last night hadn't been some twisted nightmare. I knew it hadn't. It was too real, too vivid. The pain certainly was real, and the image of Lily's broken neck would be branded into my brain for the rest of my life. Then I noticed Lily wasn't with her.

"Where's Lily?" I shouted, and then it was Stephanie's turn to recoil and step back in fear.

"She's... she's in the car... Brandon, you're scaring the shit out of me. What the hell happened? And why are you here? You're supposed to be at your painting-thing."

I didn't reply, instead barging past her, almost knocking her over. I saw Stephanie's silver Yaris in the driveway. The passenger door was open, and there was Lily, sitting happily in her baby seat. I picked her up and held her close to me, and my heart lifted like a helium balloon that had escaped a child's grasp.

"Daddy! I missed you!" she sang in her sweet voice.

"I missed you so much too, sweetie!" My relief was evident on my face as tears streamed down, wetting Lily's soft blonde hair. So it wasn't real? While holding her close to my chest, I tried to work out what had actually happened. I remembered leaving my hotel, driving home, and then seeing Lily's dead body, as if they were all as real as each other. I walked back into the house with Lily in my arms and sat her down on the settee. Stephanie was in the kitchen, starting to tidy up.

"So, you need to tell me what the hell that was," she said in a firm tone. I told her everything. Stephanie's expression became more concerned as I went on, her frown causing the creases on her forehead that I found endearing, but that she always worried were going to make her look old before she was.

"It must've been a nightmare. Lily and I are both fine, of course. You've been stressed a lot recently. It's obviously just built up and piled over." I wanted to accept her explanation, but my throbbing hand wouldn't let me.

"Where were you, anyway?" I asked her. "Maybe I dreamt everything, some kind of night terror or something, but you definitely weren't here all night."

"We were at my mum's," Stephanie replied, breaking eye contact with me. I found this strange. Stephanie and her mum had always had a difficult relationship. Her parents had separated when she was eight. Her mother, Stacey Collins, had told her that Richard (also Collins, Stacey had been happy to lose her maiden name, Badcock, a name for which she had received much ridicule, as one might imagine), her father, had wanted nothing more to do with her, and had deserted them. When Stephanie was twenty-four, she had found her father through the internet. It turned out that it was actually her mother who had had an affair and wouldn't allow Richard any contact in an attempt to keep her secret from her daughter. Stephanie was devastated when she found out, especially when, a year after her first contact with Richard, he was killed in a tragic hit and run by a drunk driver. The accident brought Stephanie and Stacey a little closer, but it was normal still for many months to pass in between them seeing each other.

"Why were you at your mum's?"

"Well, you said you were going to be at your painting retreat in Brighton all weekend, and I didn't wanna be alone. Why were you here?"

"It didn't help. I sat on the beach for eight hours, got through four different canvases, and still couldn't do anything I was proud of." It had been a few months since I'd sold any of my artwork, and the trip was Stephanie's idea. She had been the main earner in the house. Her job as a corporate lawyer was enough to cover all our expenses, but we had little left over unless I managed to sell my work.

"Something has to work soon. I've been working so hard, and I just feel like you're not contributing enough." This was a familiar argument. I'd been trying really hard, but sooner or later I would have to give it up and try and get a job. Stephanie left the room and went upstairs with Lily to unpack her and Lily's things. I hadn't told Stephanie about the calls I made to her, I realised, or the voicemail.

I'm not proud of it, but I had to check her phone. It was the only thing I could think of to find out whether any of this had been real or not. I took the phone and saw that it was on, and there weren't any missed calls displayed in the notification area, but I still wasn't convinced. I opened her contacts app, called the voicemail number, and listened to her messages. There was a message that was over a minute long from my number. I called her phone again from my own to listen to the pre-recorded voicemail message, and it was the one I was used to.

"Hi! This is Stephanie Chapman. Leave a message and I'll get back to you." Now I was starting to doubt anything that had happened. Feeling stupid, I was about to put her phone back in her bag when it vibrated in my hand. It was a text from her mum. I opened it, as if it was something hurtful from her mum (they often were). I wanted to press delete before Stephanie saw it. I read the message over and over and couldn't believe my eyes. I read it so many times that the words seemed to merge together on the screen. The only thing I was sure of now was that it was definitely not from her mother.

# CHAPTER THREE

Alice woke up in her single bed, her head still on Niel's chest. A small puddle of her dribble had collected between his pecs. She realised she was still naked, and despite everything that she and Niel had shared the night before, she was embarrassed. She managed to sit up, grab a t-shirt from the table and slip it on without disturbing Niel's sleep. She couldn't help but look at him while he slept. He was so *gorgeous*. Even with his hair in its post-sex and sleep mess, she couldn't imagine a more perfect looking man. That wasn't the reason she had completely fallen for him, of course. He was such a generous lover. She was almost in a sex-induced coma before Niel had finished. She knew straight away that sex with any other man would never compare to Niel. It was as if he could feel everything that he was making her feel. How else could he have known exactly what to do, and exactly when to do it? While she was happily reliving the previous night's activities, Niel woke up.

"Good morning Alice," he said. He smiled that wonderful smile, displaying his perfect teeth.

"Good morning," Alice replied softly, realising she had put a top on, but was still naked on her bottom half, and blushed. Niel rummaged around on the bed, found Alice's underwear, and handed it to her. *This man really can read my mind,* Alice mused, then put on her underwear under the cover.

They spent what Alice could only describe as a wonderfully long time kissing, the tongues intertwining and circling one another, Alice's passion and arousal that she thought had been spent the previous night reigniting.

"What are you doing today?" Niel asked, and Alice thought he was looking for an excuse to leave.

"Umm. It's my mum's birthday. I'm going back home, staying there tonight, seeing friends tomorrow, then coming back tomorrow night."

"Oh, cool! Where's home?"

"A small village, not too far from here," Alice replied her rehearsed response. She didn't usually bother giving the name of the village, Alconbury, as she knew everyone usually responded with, *where's that?*

"A village? Nice, never been to a village before. I'm from London myself. Is there a village idiot?" Niel asked, chuckling to himself. Alice could think of several. They spoke for a couple of hours, from their friends back home, to the kinds of food they both liked and didn't like, their favourite films, and a lot of things in between. She was worried that a lot of the things they spoke about, they didn't match on. Niel loved spicy food. Alice couldn't even eat a korma. Niel loved horror films, especially *The Exorcist*, as that was the only horror film, according to him, that had actually scared him. Alice likes romantic comedy films. This worried her a little, but again, as if he could read her mind, Niel said, "I've always believed opposites attract anyway," and kissed her on the nose.

Alice had temporarily forgotten that she needed to catch a bus at 12:25. At 11:40 she realised she didn't have much time and told Niel that she had to get ready now. Luckily, the bus stop was only five minutes away from her place, but she hadn't packed a bag yet.

"I know we only met last night, and... and it's probably really presumptuous, maybe even rude of me to ask, but I couldn't come with you, could I? It's just that, I don't really wanna go back to my place and not be with you all weekend." Alice thought that he had to be psychic or something. She didn't want to be without him either, but was way too shy to ask if he wanted to go.

"That would be great. I'm sure my mum will love you. Especially since you're from London. She'll be asking you all sorts of embarrassing questions though, probably!"

"Well, why don't you get ready? I'm gonna go grab some stuff and sort out this state." He said, pointing at his hair. "I'll meet you outside your building in fifteen?" Alice agreed. As quick as she could, she tied up her hair, knowing she didn't have time to wash it. The showers in her student accommodation were pathetic. To say it trickled would be being generous.

As Alice was standing in the shower, she started to feel dizzy and lightheaded, and her head lolled from side to side. Bright spots appeared in front of both of her eyes, as if someone had taken a photo of her with the flash on in the dark. The spots grew, gradually filling her vision. Alice leaned against the wall and felt her knees go weak. The white turned to black, and Alice collapsed to the bottom of the bathtub, urine flowing from between her legs, the shower practically dripping onto her hair. The next thing she knew, she was on the bus with Niel.

"Niel? What happened? I was just... I was at home..."

"What are you talking about? We've been on the bus for twenty minutes, Alice." They were sitting together on the front seats of the bus. Alice looked out through the windscreen and noticed that they were veering onto the wrong side of the road. An arctic lorry was on the other side. There was nowhere to turn, and it seemed as though neither of the drivers had time to stop. The front of the lorry came into contact with the right-hand-side of the front of their bus. Metal on both vehicles crumpled into one another. The bus didn't have seatbelts, and everyone riding it was flung forward. The old lady at the back collided head first with a handrail, crushing her neck. The lorry continued its journey through the bus, killing everyone on the right-hand-side. Alice and Niel were sitting on the left, at the front, Niel was in an aisle seat, Alice the window. Niel was also catapulted from his seat, and collided with the windscreen, before shattering it and landing on the road. Alice was lucky; her body was thrown to the right, where she collided with another passenger, cracking two of her ribs. She might not have described herself as lucky in that moment, but as she regained consciousness and looked around the bus, tasting the tang of blood in her mouth, she realised in horror that she was the only passenger who wasn't either dead, or unconscious. Several limbs were scattered around the bus, separated from their owners. There it was again, that bright white spot, in front of both eyes, following her gaze. Again, they grew, and when Alice regained her sight, she was back in the shower.

After regaining her composure from what was the most vivid nightmare she'd ever had—no, not nightmare - vision, she got out of the shower and walked over to the mirror. There was a strong taste of iron in her mouth, but when she spat, nothing - no blood. Her right side also ached, but she could see no sign of bruising, or the telltale sign of a broken rib protruding through her skin. Shaken, and if she was honest, very scared, she continued to get ready. She saw the time and realised she had only two more minutes to get ready. She upturned her backpack onto the floor, threw some clothes and some make-up into her bag and left. Niel was outside of her building, as he said he would be, when she got outside. On the walk to the bus stop Alice told her new lover about the experience she had had while she was in the shower, and when the bus pulled up to the stop, Niel being the gentleman he was, insisted that she get on first. Setting her foot onto the first step, Alice's mind raced with flashbacks from her vision - she didn't want to get on the bus. It was irrational, she knew that, but seeing Niel getting horrifically injured once already was enough for one day, one lifetime, in fact.

"Alice, it was just a bad dream, or something like that. I'm sure it'll be fine. I mean, how many times have you taken this bus and nothing has happened?"

"I'm sorry, but I can't," Alice said, stepping back down from the bus. Niel was frustrated with her until he saw the tears rolling down her cheeks.

"OK don't worry! We don't have to go, Alice, we can just stay at your place, and I'll help you forget this happened, if you know what I mean," Niel said in an attempt to cheer her up. Fresh tears started on their journey from Alice's eyes, as she really wanted to see her mum for her birthday.

"Tell you what," Niel offered as a compromise, "I'll drive us there. Would you be happy with that?"

Alice was, of course, happy with that. Niel did own a car, but he doesn't enjoy driving, not one bit. When Alice previously mentioned going by bus, Niel was relieved. He'd never been involved in a car accident of any kind, nor even witnessed one, so perhaps it could be described as an irrational fear. Still, fear is fear, and he avoided sitting behind the wheel as much as he could. But spending the whole weekend with Alice? That was definitely worth driving for, he decided. They took the short walk over to his place, round the back of the building to the car park and climbed into his VW Polo. Not exactly a boy racer, Alice decided immediately, and was pleased at that. When a new McDonald's had opened up in the nearest town to Alice's home, a 'gang' of boy racers used to take over the car park after darkness fell, pulling doughnuts and generally being, as described by her friends, 'McMorons'. She was certain she couldn't be with a bloke who was a McMoron.

Despite having taken this journey many times by bus, and a couple in her mum's car, Alice wasn't sure of the exact way to get back home. Niel, displaying his great level of patience, pulled up alongside the road before the bus stop they were planning on using earlier, killed the engine and waited for another bus to arrive. The wait was about half an hour, during which time, well, you can probably guess what Alice and Niel did to fill the time; lots of 'making out', as it was becoming popularly known, probably due to the increase of American TV making its way onto English television sets. Soon the bus arrived, collected the waiting passengers and departed. Niel started the car and followed the bus along its entire journey.

Forty-seven minutes later (there had been traffic), the Polo entered the small village of Alconbury. Alice stole a quick kiss from Niel, then they made their way across the lawn (which her mother, Julie Hamilton, would later scold Alice for, she was old enough to know better, *there's a path for a reason, you know*). She'd heard that a dozen times if she'd heard it once. Niel was distracting her, however, and her mind was in other, happy places, rather than worrying about her mother's lawn.

"Ali! Good to see you, sugar lump. How are you?" Julie asked her only child. She had wanted more children, Kevin, her husband, had not, so they had compromised, and had one child, and a dog. A pug that had been Alice's best, and at times, only friend growing up, had died before Alice reached puberty, a loss that took her many months to recover from. Julie was forty-three, but was told by most people that she met that she looked at least fifteen years younger. Much to her delight, she even still got asked for ID occasionally.

"Hi Mummy. Happy birthday!" Alice gleamed.

"Now now. Who's this handsome young man you have with you?" Julie couldn't hide her delight at seeing her daughter with a man, *and what a man!* she thought to herself.

"Hi Mrs Hamilton, it's a pleasure to meet you. I'm Niel, Alice's..." he looked at Alice, saw her smile, and ended the sentence with, "boyfriend." Niel wondered if they were official now. He hoped so. It had only been a day (well, not even a whole twenty-four hours, actually), but he had never had such strong feelings for a girl before, and he had been with a few.

"Pleasure to meet you too, Niel. Please come in." Julie gestured towards the open front door.

"After you, please." Niel allowed both Alice and Julie to go ahead of him, in a true display of gentlemanly behaviour, Julie thought, and she liked him already. They walked together through to the sitting room. It was luxurious, adorned with mahogany furniture, thick wool carpet, exposed black ceiling beams andcream walls. Niel smiled at the numerous family photos lovingly displayed on every available surface.

"Mummy, can I get you a drrrrrrrrr....," was all Alice managed to say before she collapsed onto the floor.

# CHAPTER FOUR

## BRANDON

I stared at the phone in shock and disbelief. Stephanie must have saved this person's number as *Mum* to hide it from me. What I saw almost made me vomit on the spot.

*Hey babe, last night was fucking amazing. You should definitely 'visit your mum' more often, haha. Talk soon, yea? Xxx.*

I was gripping the phone so tightly I'm surprised it didn't shatter in my hand. My heart felt as though it was being fed into a giant paper shredder. Stephanie and I had been married for two years, and we were together for two years before that, and during that time I'd never once considered she would cheat on me.

We'd met at an art exhibit on one of the rare occasions when I had managed to get some of my work displayed. I had painted a scene of the Houses of Parliament from across the Thames, the water glistening in the foreground, the sky black with smoke from the fire that was raging through Parliament. The idea had come to me one day whilst I was walking through London. I had overheard a tourist complaining about how they never saw any police officers in London, and that it was no wonder it was such a dangerous place. Having lived here most of my life, and having experienced no danger whatsoever, I decided to paint a piece to demonstrate how bad things could be if there were no police, no defence. I'd always thought that ignorance caused you to not be able to tell how green the grass is on one's side. Anyway, this is how I explained my artwork to the most beautiful woman I'd ever seen in my life, and also the first person to pay my work any attention that day. Her pale white skin and dark black hair created a more beautiful contrast than any I'd ever managed in my artwork. She stood at the perfect height (in my opinion) of five foot four, making my five foot nine not as short as I'd always considered it to be.

She made me feel a confidence I'd never felt before, and without even being completely aware of it, I asked her, "Well, if I manage to sell this piece today, how about I take you out? Dinner, then drinks?"

"Sounds good to me. I know a wonderful Italian."

She smiled a beautiful smile at me, while brushing her shoulder length glossy black hair behind her ear. Before turning and heading over to see the other exhibits, she handed me her business card. The gallery was closing at 5pm, and by 4 o'clock the image of a romantic Italian meal with Stephanie was fading away. That was until the gallery manager, Josef, approached me, shook my hand, and offered me a cheque for £2,000. My piece had sold, and Stephanie and I met at *Locanda Locatelli*, a wonderful looking Michelin-starred restaurant that I'd never heard of, but the reviews I had read on my phone while on the way there spoke nothing but praise.

Stephanie wore a figure hugging black dress and seemed a million miles out of my league. Yet still, there she was, sitting opposite me, staring into my eyes, lust and interest in my every word painted across her beautiful face. Our first courses arrived. A plate of creamy, salted cod was placed expertly onto Stephanie's side of the table by the young Italian waiter, before deep-fried mozzarella and a tomato salad arrived at mine. We ate and enjoyed each other's company for the next couple of hours, and we both felt as if we'd known each other for years. By the time we actually had, things weren't quite as perfect as they had been that night. Stephanie had always been the main earner out of the two of us. Her career took its toll on her, and every evening when she came home and asked what I'd managed to do that day, her stress was exacerbated. When Lily came along, it became my job to be the househusband, and my artwork from then on was even less successful than it had been previously.

"Brandon, do you..." Stephanie asked, trailing off as she saw my tear-stained face, and she realised what had happened.

"Baby, I... I'm so sorry. I've been so stressed, and... and..." I didn't give her a chance to explain herself. I dropped the phone and headed for the door. On my way out, I caught a glimpse of the painting that Stephanie had proudly displayed on the sitting room wall, a painting of the Houses of Parliament aflame. The door closed firmly behind me, and I walked into a sheet of heavy rain, the dark clouds emulating my mood. I hadn't thought to bring a coat, and my grey shirt that I'd been wearing since the day before stuck to every inch of my upper body. I looked down at myself whilst wandering aimlessly and wondered when I had become so rotund. No wonder Stephanie had resorted to looking elsewhere for sexual satisfaction. I hadn't visited a gym for a long time. I'd convinced myself that I didn't have time since Lily came along. My mind fought its way through so many thoughts, much like a commuter facing the crowds of London rush hour on the tube, how I must have not been satisfying Stephanie in the bedroom, how I've been taking how much work she does for granted, and how I don't understand how hard she works. I soon found myself in the location of the metaphor - the Stratford Tube Station, a twenty-five-minute walk from the house I shared with Stephanie, a journey that I still don't remember to this day. Without even realising it, I had stopped at a local newsagent and bought four Polish lagers. I sat outside the station, drinking and watching all the happy people walk past, many of them couples, mocking me with their happiness and love. My phone rang. I pulled it out of my pocket, and the contact picture for Stephanie was on the screen - the pair of us, cheek to cheek, smiling in front of the Eifel tower, from the trip to France Stephanie surprised me with for my 29th birthday. Many missed calls, and several lagers later, I decided to answer.

"Babe, thank God. Where are you? I'm so sorry. Tell me where you are," Stephanie pleaded. It was the same voice that had spoken so softly to me in our bed, that had told me how much she loved me. It was the same one that had shouted at me after a long day of work, as I was often the only outlet for the stress that built up in her daily. Listening to her now through my phone, I felt nothing. I would've preferred to be on the end of one of her shouting episodes. At least I would have still felt something for her.

"Do you care where I am? Did you care where I was when you were with that *motherfucker*?!" I spat into my phone.

"Of course I care!" I could hear the crack in her voice as she fought back tears. "I love you. I just... made a mistake, that's all."

"How many times? How many times? How long have you been seeing him? Who is he?"

"Come back home, baby, and we can talk about it. I don't wanna talk about this over the phone. Come back to me and Lily and we'll sort all of this out, OK?"

"Don't bring Lily into this! I can't talk to you right now. I'll call you when I can get the image of you fucking another guy out of my head, so don't expect to hear from me anytime soon," I almost screamed, and then hung up the call. I finished the last of my four pack, my need for alcohol not at all satiated. Many people walked past me. The morning rush-hour was in full swing, and I could feel them deliberately avoiding looking in my direction.

I managed to gather my composure and rise to my feet; the alcohol was affecting me more than I thought, and walked without aim or purpose. Some time later, I found myself at a park near West Ham Tube Station. I must have walked for nearly an hour, though time had no meaning to me in this state of mind. There was a bench by some trees, completely deserted on a Monday morning, the perfect spot to ignore the world and be alone in the dungeon of my thoughts. The sunlight found its way through a gap in the clouds, the warm rays sending me into an ocean of dreams of betrayal and horrifying phone calls from Stephanie, speaking in the terrible voice that she had the night before.

"Brandon!" A voice woke me, and as I forced my eyes open I was surprised to see a man I didn't know sitting next to me on the bench. "Women, huh?" he said in a deep voice.

"I'm sorry, do I know you?"

"They're all the same, aren't they? Can't trust a single one of 'em." He spoke without looking at me, staring into the ground as if contemplating his own problems.

"I wouldn't know what you're talking about," I replied, still wondering who this guy was and how he knew me.

"Brandon, come on. If we're gonna be friends, and we are going to be *such* close friends, you gotta be honest with me. That Stephanie is such a *bitch*, am I right?"

Now I had progressed from curious and a little frightened to perplexed and genuinely afraid. Who was this bloke? Was he the one that had been having an affair with her? How else could he know what he knew? I stood up to my full, although not considerable height, and stared straight at him, though he still wasn't looking at me. "Are you the prick who has been seeing my wife?" I asked him. I couldn't say *fucking*; the word would have created too strong an image in the catalogue of thoughts my mind was currently flicking through.

"Now Brandon, if we're going to be such good friends, why would I want to *see* your wife?"

"Then who the fuck are you?!" I was getting angry now, an emotion I rarely express. This man, though, definitely had a way of encouraging it.

"I keep telling you, Brandon, I'm your friend. I'm probably going to be the closest thing you have to one soon, anyway." Still, he hadn't looked at me, his gaze was fixed on the floor. "And what do friends do for each other, Brandon? They help each other out, right? I'm gonna help you out with this problem with your wife."

"And how, exactly, are you going to do that? Look at me! I said *look* at me!" Still, he didn't.

"I happen to know who your wife has been seeing, Brandon. I know who he is, I know where he is. I also know that your wife has been seeing him for a year now, Brandon. A whole year. This wasn't some one night thing that she can blame on alcohol. They *planned* to see each other, to deceive you, to *betray* you." Though he still wasn't looking at me, I could see the smile spreading across his face. It wasn't a nice smile. It almost seemed evil, as if he knew he was in a position of power.

"Who is he? *Tell me.*" I was more than angry by now. I could feel my every pulse sending rage through my arteries. My fists were clenched so hard that my nails almost drew blood in the palms of my hands, and I could almost see my anger, a red haze in front of my eyes.

"Before I tell you, Brandon, I need to know what you're going to do about this. If you're just gonna shout your mouth off at him and nothing more - well, *no deal.*" I didn't even think about this. In my rage fuelled state I wasn't capable of logical thought, my usually calm and collected demeanour replaced by a new side of me that this unknown man had created.

"I'm going to kill him." This thought scared me initially. I'd never hurt anyone in my life and certainly hadn't thought about killing anyone. But the idea was planted in my mind and grew until it overshadowed other thoughts.

"*Good*, Brandon. Good. That's what people like him deserve. His name is Robert Fields. He's forty-two, and he works at Taylor and Bennett's law with your deceitful wife." I knew Robert. Well, I'd met him, briefly, at Stephanie's office Christmas party. Thinking back, he did seem to be avoiding Stephanie and me when we were together. I saw him talking with Stephanie on a couple of occasions that night, and when I returned to her, he made an excuse and left her to speak with someone else. He was a good-looking bastard, too. He stood at least four inches taller than me, had defined muscles rather than barely used ones resting under a layer of fat like me, and his greying hair matched his tanned skin perfectly.

"So how are you going to do it?" the man asked, after finally making eye contact with me for the first time.

# CHAPTER FIVE

## ALICE

A series of memories passed through Alice's subconscious as if they were being shown through an old-style film projector. Each came and went before she had time to process them; primary school, secondary school. birthdays, a couple of weddings, a funeral, starting university, Niel. The image of Niel remained in her mind, his beautiful face smiling at her, a light in the dark depths of her subconscious. Now they were in his car, the bright sunshine that had warmed the day was gone, night had fallen, wrapping their surroundings in its sombre cloak. Niel was still smiling that wonderful smile at Alice, and she started to worry that he should keep his eyes on the road rather than on her. The road they were on came into her vision, she knew that it was near her mother's home. She'd been on this road many times, but as more details of her surroundings came to her, the less like that road it became. The easy, simple beauty of the surroundings she was so familiar with were twisted into a distorted version of the reality that she knew from growing up in the village. Instead of flowers growing on the verges of the road, winding, violent looking vines wrapped around each other, giant thorns pointing in all directions. As the headlights of Niel's car shone onto the trees that ominously surrounded the road on both sides, Alice could have sworn that the gnarled trunks of the old trees had faces, features wrought out of bark, that glared at her as they passed them by.

Niel seemed totally unaware of the things that were frightening Alice, and he drove along the road, the surface of which reminded Alice of the acne-ridden face of a boy she knew from school. The further down the road they went, the narrower the road became, or so Alice thought. She became aware that Niel was talking to her, she could see his lips moving, could hear his voice, but couldn't understand anything he was saying, her mind unable to focus on anything other than the dark, oppressive woodland threatening to swallow the car whole.

The vision of being in Niel's car began to fade, the lights illuminating the road ahead being dimmed until she was floating in a world of nothing but blackness. A scream tried to escape from her lips, but it fell silent into the void. She walked, though her feet touched nothing, searching for something, anything other than the suffocating darkness. There was something amid all of this nothingness, she knew, and she wanted to find it. She walked, step after step, with no idea for how long she had been walking. Slowly, a mass of contorted thorny vines started to appear, above her, below her, all around her, following her.

The vines seemed to have a collective pulse, beating in rhythm with her own heart, a thick black substance pumping, coursing through them, provoking the thorns to leak the black sludge. Looking at the gunk filled Alice with an unexplainable fear, as if just looking at it could harm her. She became aware of another presence nearby, in this world that she could only describe as purgatory. Though she couldn't see anyone, she spoke out to it. "What do you want from me? Where am I?" The fear was evident in the shaking of her voice.

"I don't want anything from you," a voice answered, from everywhere and nowhere, from inside her head and from the vines encircling her. "But you will want something from me."

"I don't want to be here. Please, let me go…" Alice's voiced cracked as the vines grew closer and closer, the menacing, evil blackness they excreted now terrifying her, leaving her no way of escaping this world. Alice now felt totally powerless. She had never believed in fate and preferred to believe that she could carve her own path. The scales of her own life had always been kept in relative balance, her standing on one side, the other with her goals and wishes for her future. In this new world of black though, the scales were not balanced, the black sludge weighing her down, tipping the scales so that her aspirations moved impossibly out of her reach, her entire belief system in shatters.

"You'll ask for my help soon," the voice boomed, echoing through her entire being. "When you enter the pit of despair, only I will be there to pull you back out. You will need my help with Niel, I promise you." Before Alice could question what this meant, she was pulled out of this world, and felt as though she were being rescued from drowning, gasping for breath. The light burnt her eyes as if she was opening them for the first time, until she was able to make out the faces of Niel, Julie and Kevin.

"Alice! Are you OK?" Julie and Niel almost screamed in harmony, the concern etched onto their faces. Alice tried to answer, but instead turned her head to one side and vomited all over the cream carpet.

"Let's take you to the bathroom," Kevin said, putting Alice's arm round his shoulder. He helped her to the bathroom, pushed her hair back behind her ears and washed her face with a warm flannel.

"So, want to tell your old man what's going on, poppet?"

"I don't know Daddy. Maybe I'm stressed from university." She didn't tell him about what she had seen while collapsed on the floor, though she knew she'd never forget it. The thought of the creeping vines made her shudder all over.

"Let's take you upstairs. Nothing a little nap won't fix".

Niel took Alice up to her room, helped her undress and got her into bed.

"Are you OK, Alice? I'm really worried about you. You were out for like five minutes. Has that ever happened before?" Niel asked. She told him about how she collapsed in the shower earlier that morning, and Niel became more and more worried as she went on.

"Your dad is probably right. Get some sleep and come down when you feel better, OK?"

"OK. Are you sure you'll be alright on your own with my parents, though?" Alice asked, worried.

"They seem really nice. I'm sure it'll be fine. Don't worry." Niel kissed her on the forehead, turned to leave the room, and blew her a kiss before closing the door.

Alice awoke some time later and could hear the familiar sound of her mother laughing downstairs, the endearing telltale snort as she gasped for breath while laughing echoing up the stairs. She found her top and jeans and dressed before looking in the mirror. Her hair was wild from sleep, and she spent some time using her old hair brush that had been left on her make-up table to try to make herself look presentable. *What does Niel see in me?* Alice asked the mirror. Even the most optimistic of people have moments of self-doubt, and Alice, ever the pessimist, genuinely had no idea why Niel had chosen her over the ridiculously curvy Megan or the beautiful Charlie, when either of her two friends would've happily swapped places with Alice when she took him home last night. Another snort from downstairs distracted Alice from herself, and she hurried downstairs to join Niel and her parents.

"Hey Alice! How are you feeling now?" Niel got up to welcome Alice into the room and embraced her. His strong, muscular arms made Alice feel so safe, and if her parents weren't in the room, she wouldn't have let go of him for anything.

"I think I'm OK. Sorry, everyone. I don't know what happened." She looked down at the carpet, the orange stain visible against the cream colour, and her cheeks flushed red.

"Don't worry, petal," Julie said reassuringly. "We know a lovely young man down the road that can clean it for us. We're just glad that you're okay now."

Alice wasn't sure that she was okay. She'd never passed out before and had never had such vivid, intense dreams before today. She was still shaking from the image of being trapped by the vines, the awful black substance that possessed such an evil aura, and the... man? Was he a man? Was he even human? The presence that had spoken to her about Niel. She dismissed the thoughts and brought herself back out of the catacombs of her mind.

"I'll be fine thank you Mummy," Alice said, and suddenly remembered the present that she was holding and handed it to Julie.

"Happy birthday!" Alice beamed. Julie thanked her, and carefully opened the present, trying her best not to tear the paper, which Alice knew she would keep for some reason. As the paper was removed and the *Fat Face* logo was revealed, Julie got up and hugged Alice without even knowing what was inside, the fact that it was from *Fat Face* was enough for Julie. She resumed opening the present, finding a colourful necklace, matching bracelet and a jumper with similar colours. After Julie had put all of her presents on, Niel pulled a small box out of his pocket and handed it to Julie.

"I got you a little something too, Mrs Hamilton."

"Oh, Niel! You shouldn't have!" Julie gushed. "And please, I told you already. Call me Julie," she said through a smile. She opened the box and two silver earrings shone back at her, the stones elegantly set into them beautifully reflecting more light than it seemed was even in the room.

"This is too much Niel. Are you sure?" Julie asked, even though she was already putting them on.

"Of course, happy birthday!" Kevin heaved himself out of his chair, his bulk obviously causing him difficulty in standing up, and shook Niel's hand.

"You're a good man, Niel. I'm glad Alice managed to find a man like her father!" he joked, his belly jiggling with his laughter.

Julie was glad her parents were taking such a liking to Niel, but was really shocked by the present he'd got for Julie. He must've bought it while she was in the shower this morning, she thought. Still, as he'd never met her parents, and had only met Alice herself the night before, it was a little strange she couldn't help but think. She was ashamed of herself for thinking it, but couldn't help feeling a little shown up, as his present had definitely cost more than her own.

Through the rest of the day, they ate together. Julie's homemade cake was delicious as ever, and they shared a bottle of champagne, before Alice and Julie moved onto wine, and Niel and Kevin onto beer. As Julie poured out stories of what had happened in the village while she'd been away, seemingly unaware of Alice's lack of interest, Kevin and Niel shared stories of their own, often laughing at each other's jokes. Alice couldn't make out what they were talking about, but seeing them get on so well warmed her heart. Before any of them knew it, it was midnight, and both couples retired to their own rooms.

"Cute room," Niel said with a grin, as he walked into Alice's room that hadn't changed since she'd been at school. Posters of bands that she'd liked covered the walls, teddies and other various soft toys sat on all surfaces, turned to face the bed, as if keeping a watchful eye over their owner. Alice wondered if they missed her like she had missed them.

"It's so embarrassing!" Alice said, feeling her cheeks fill with blood, displaying her embarrassment. "I can't believe they kept it like this. I think Daddy wanted to change it into an office, but I guess Mummy wouldn't let him." Alice realised that she was still calling them Mummy and Daddy in front of her new partner, a habit she'd never been able to break, and felt her cheeks redden further.

"Aww, don't worry about it. My parents haven't changed mine either. They even left the girlie magazines that I'd forgotten about in there, I nearly died when I went home last time and saw them sat in a pile on my desk," Niel said with a chuckle while hugging Alice, trying to lessen her embarrassment. They sat on her bed and pressed their lips together, then opened their mouths and encircled each other's tongues with their own, tasting each other's alcohol infused breath.

"You didn't need to get my mum anything, especially not something so expensive," Alice said, when they momentarily managed to separate themselves from each other.

"Oh, it was nothing. To tell you the truth, my grandparents died recently, and left me, well, without going into too much detail, a lot of money. And anyway, I wanted to make a good impression."

"Well, that was really sweet of you, thank you. Can I tell you something, Niel?"

"Of course, beautiful."

"I've always wanted to have a boy in my room," she said, with a shy smile on her face.

"You haven't had a guy in here before, have you?" Niel asked, genuinely surprised that a girl as stunning as Alice hadn't snuck a guy up here before, though he was certain that there must have been many who wished they had been in his own position right now. Alice shook her head. Though she was still smiling broadly, she was unable to make eye contact with him, her shyness taking over. Niel placed two fingers under Alice's chin, lifted her head, and looked into her beautiful blue eyes.

"Well, I'm honoured to be the first." They kissed and made love through the night, and in between immense tidal waves of pleasure, Alice was unable to keep her thoughts from the vision, or nightmare, or whatever it was that she'd experienced earlier. She couldn't shake the feeling that the presence in the dark world was still around her somehow, and what it had said to her. Why did it tell her that she would need help with Niel? What did it know that she didn't?

# CHAPTER SIX

## BRANDON

I now sat alone on the bench, still soaking wet, my new 'friend' having left me alone. Passers-by looked at me with from under their umbrellas with either sympathy or bemusement. I was so enveloped in my own thoughts that I didn't feel the cold. It had drifted to scenes of Stephanie and Robert aggressively fucking each other, and then to Robert and me, with me aggressively beating the life out of him. These were thoughts and feelings that I had never experienced before, but imagining the things that I would do to Robert was my only source of some kind of happiness at that moment. I told my 'friend' - I call him this as that's the only name I had for him, and he seemed to be on my side - that I would kill Robert, but now that he was gone, I really didn't think that I would be capable of doing so. Surely I had to do something though, otherwise, would their affair really stop? Sure, I could go home to Stephanie, forgive her. We'd move on from it, but it could start again in the future. I needed to confront him, tell him I know, maybe threaten to tell his wife, but *killing him*? I've never even punched anyone and felt not only ridiculous but frankly a little scared of myself for having such thoughts. I looked at my watch and was surprised to see that it was almost midday. The rain was showing mercy and had stopped, though as English weather can be ever so fickle, it probably wouldn't be long before it started again.

Managing to stand up from the bench, my hair still dripping, I pulled my phone out of my pocket, and saw more missed calls from Stephanie, along with twelve text messages, all along the lines of *I'm sorry* and *please come home*. I put the phone back in my pocket, swore under my breath, and tried to decide what to do next. I don't have many friends - in fact there is only one person that I would describe as such. Steve Foster and I had been friends at school, the fact that neither of us had any other friends drew us together. He was often ridiculed for his ginger hair, just as I was bullied for everything from having no parents to being gay, even though I wasn't. Steve was now a fairly well respected art critic, and it was only thanks to him that I had ever sold any of my pieces.

I didn't want to disturb him with my marital problems and felt that even he would have a hard time believing everything else that had happened to me. So I was alone in the world, with nobody to talk to, not even my new 'friend'. Again I walked, with no purpose or destination, my subconscious steering me until I eventually ended up at Plaistow tube station, trying to go through the ticket gate. The machine beeped at me over and over, no matter how many times I touched my Oyster card to the reader.

"Sir, can you please step away from the gate? You need to top up your card," the station worker told me. He was young, twenty at most I guessed, and his annoyance at me holding people up and forming a queue behind me was evident through the paper thin customer service façade.

"Sorry," I muttered and pushed back through the queue I had created to add a tenner to my card. Once the card was topped up, I tried again to get through the gates to the platforms, successfully this time, and walked down the wet, slippery steps to the ancient platform that was badly in need of refurbishment. A train pulled up at the platform, surprisingly full for this time of day, and I boarded without looking at anyone onboard, as is customary in London. The last time I made eye contact with anyone on the Tube, I nearly got into a fight.

The next thing I knew, I was getting off the Tube half an hour later at Westminster. Of course, it was raining again, in sheets now. As I crossed Westminster Bridge, the Thames below my feet was higher than I'd ever seen it, mere feet from the surface of the man-made river banks. Still, I walked, past St Thomas Hospital on my right, various pubs on my left, until I came to a nearby cheap hotel. I was tired and soaking wet, so made my way inside. The bar offered surprisingly cheap beer for London at £4.20 a pint, so I sat, ordering a second before I had finished the dregs of the first. It was 2:30 in the afternoon now, so why not, I thought. The barman didn't need to know that it wasn't my first drink of the day. The alcohol started to affect me, and my eyelids felt so heavy that they were weighing the rest of my head down. I staggered over to the reception desk and booked a room for the night. I paid using our joint debit card, knowing that Stephanie wouldn't berate me about the £129 room. After all, how many times has she spent nights in hotels like this with that smug bastard Robert? The room was warm, and as soon as I peeled off my clothes and placed them over the heater, I collapsed into a deep sleep on the surprisingly comfortable queen bed. My 'friend' entered my dreams and reminded me of how much I hated Robert, how much I wanted him dead. When I woke with fresh feelings of rage, I dressed into my now almost dry clothes, checked my watch and realised I had slept for four hours, and headed back out onto the streets of London.

"Any change, guv?" a man sitting on the side of the road outside my hotel asked me.

"No," I replied, my mood allowing me no sympathy.

"Fuck you then, prick," he shouted back, and I fought the urge to turn back and confront him.

I boarded the Jubilee line tube, fully conscious this time, with a destination in mind.

By the time I climbed the stairs back out onto the street in Canary Wharf, the rain had once again stopped, the sun taking one of few opportunities today to shine through the gaps in the clouds and warm my skin. My mood was still much darker than any of the clouds hanging overhead, ready to reclaim the sky as I walked the familiar route to the offices of Taylor and Bennett. Stephanie was rarely home before eight, but she wasn't at work today. I was sure that Robert would be, though. I looked around and found a pillar a short distance away from the main doors to the building, off to the side, so I could lean and wait for the bastard to leave work. Half an hour later, I laid eyes on the smug-looking high-flying son of a bitch. Every part of him screamed success; the designer suit, leather briefcase, Italian shoes and perfect tan. He walked around the back of the building to the car park and I followed a short distance behind. He got into a stunning white Porsche and started to pull out of the car park. Luckily, at that same moment, a black London taxi drew into the car park and dropped off another well-dressed grey-haired gentleman. I ran over, waving to the driver, and got into the taxi before the previous occupant had had time to close the doors.

"Hi, can you please follow the Porsche? My friend and I are having a couple of shandies tonight," I said with a fake chuckle.

"You're the boss," the cab driver replied without any humour in his voice.

The taxi journey lasted about thirty minutes, and when I got out, I produced two crumpled £20 notes from my pocket and told him to keep the change. Robert had already entered his luxurious home in the extravagant W1 area of London. I stood a few doors down, planning my next move.

I opened my eyes. When had I closed them? They felt so heavy. I was surprised to find I was in my hotel room. How had that happened? My last memory was of standing on Robert's street in the evening, and now I was on my hotel bed, my watch telling me that it was 8:30 the next morning. My phone was on the side table, and just as I picked it up to read the eighteen text messages that Stephanie had sent me, it vibrated in my hand and died. My head felt like a log that had just been split in two by a skilled lumberjack.

Every time I tried to remember what had happened the night before, the pain coursed through me, making it impossible. My knuckles, I noticed, had patches of raw, red skin, and blood had dried onto my skin and the cuffs of my shirt sleeves. My shirt had several buttons missing and hung open at my belly, and I noticed that my wallet was missing. *Shit!* Had it fallen out while I was at Robert's house? I managed to get to my feet, the room spinning around me as my head throbbed, and I entered the tiny bathroom. There were several thin streaks of blood across my face, I noticed in horror in the mirror, though when I washed it from my face and the water ran pink down the drain, there were visible cuts on my face. Was the blood mine?

Memories came flooding back to me. I was outside Robert's huge front door, knocking on it angrily. He came to the door, a confused look on his face, until his expression changed to one of fright as he appeared to recognise me. The memories subsided, and I was back in the hotel bathroom. I had no idea what was happening to me, and I dropped to the floor, my head in my hands, scratching at my temples hoping to somehow release the pain that was blotting out every other one of my senses. Robert was trying to close the door now while I was leaning against it, trying to force it open with all my strength. Normally, he looked like he would be a lot stronger than me, even though he was about twelve years my senior. However, the adrenalin and emotion surging through me gave me energy I'd never felt before, and I managed to barge the door open, knocking him to the floor. On the bathroom floor, every part of my body was screaming in agony. A noise that I could only describe as sounding like a chorus of violent thunder raged through the room until I was once again with Robert. Terrifying though these memories of what I'd done to Robert were, at least when I was experiencing them, I was away from the pain and sounds of my hotel room. I was sitting atop him now, throwing punches with both fists. He managed to block most of them, throwing my hands to the side, my knuckles scraping down the walls. The occasional blow landed on his face, causing blood and spit to erupt from his broken lips. With an impressive display of strength, Robert managed to grab my wrists and throw me off of him. Instead of attacking me, he ran into the front room.

I was sobbing in my hotel room now, my head resting on my knees, facing the corner of the room, my whole life now only consisting of constant throbbing, stabbing pain, as though I was being skewered by a team of Olympic fencers, and the sound that would've torn my eardrums apart if the sound was not coming from inside my own head. I chased Robert through the sitting room. He turned to face me, a look of fear and defiance on his face, the fire poker in his right hand, the muscles of his right arm bulging, veins thick. He threw a punch at me and connected with my left shoulder. I yelped in pain, but as he took a second swing, I caught the poker from him and threw it behind me.

"Brandon, look... I'm sorry... I know how you must feel." I could tell he was saying this through fear of what I might do to him, rather than through genuine feelings of remorse.

"No, you fucking don't. That's my *wife* you've been fucking, for a whole year! How can you say you're sorry?!"

"A year? No! We did it twice only, I swear!" His expression seemed to confirm what he was saying, but my 'friend' had told me otherwise.

"I don't give a shit. Nobody fucks my wife. Especially not you, you slimy bastard." Before he could say anything else, I was on him again.

I was screaming now, the invisible assault from the fencer's foils increasing. Blood was leaking from my ears, eyes and nose. My brain felt like it was being minced in a blender, the remains pouring from every orifice on my body. Robert's face now looked more like a plate of meatballs in tomato sauce, his own blood almost drowning him. Punch after punch I threw, yet somehow, he was still awake.

"Bran..." he managed to croak, and I relented my assault on him. He looked so pathetic now, and I looked down at him and smiled. Now he wouldn't fuck with me again, I felt sure. Though I had a sudden realisation. I couldn't leave him like this; if he survives, I'll be in deep shit. He knows who I am and there's no doubt that as soon as his wife comes home, she'll call an ambulance and then the police. I knew what I had to do. I wrapped my hands around his throat. My wedding ring shone amidst the blood on my hands, a reminder of why I was here. It reminded me why I was murdering a man with my own hands. I smiled as Robert's last breath left his broken face.

# CHAPTER SEVEN

## ALICE

Alice awoke blissfully comfortable on Niel's defined chest. She was topless herself, and as Niel woke up, he grinned at Alice's half nakedness, and he caressed her breast with the palm of his hand. The fact that it took more than one hand to cover one of her breasts turned him on greatly, and Alice could feel his arousal pressing against the inside of her thigh. Before they had time to have morning sex, Kevin knocked at the door.

"Morning both! Breakfast in 5 minutes!" he exclaimed in a happy, booming voice.

"Morning," both Alice and Niel offered in return, attempting to hide their sexual frustration. Niel threw on some fresh clothes, and Alice threw on her pyjamas, not worrying about underwear.

"How did you sleep?" asked Julie, who was already sitting at the dining table with a steaming mug of coffee.

"Very well. Thank you, Mrs Hamilton," Niel replied. "Julie, I mean. Sorry."

"Good, good. Your dad's just doing his famous fried breakfast, though I think he could do without one himself," she smiled.

"Oi oi! Less of that, cheeky!" Kevin joked, though she was right, his doctor had warned him off fried food, as his cholesterol was dangerously high.

"Smells amazing, Kev," Niel said, while Julie was quite aware that he had no trouble calling him Kev and not Mr Hamilton.

Soon Kevin had set down four plates of fantastic fried English breakfasts, very crispy bacon, proper sausages, fried Burford Brown eggs - he was very specific about those and said that he wouldn't ever buy any other eggs, beans, mushrooms and fried bread. They all ate as if they hadn't eaten in days until their plates were clean.

"We have to get going soon, Mummy. Sorry, I have so much uni work to do."

"That's OK, petal. Wouldn't want to keep you from your work." Alice was only in her first year of university, and though the final grades from that year had no bearings on her final grades, she took it very seriously. Plus, psychology interested her greatly. The topic covered such a range of fascinating aspects of human life, something that she struggled with socially.

"I'm sure you'll be fine, as long as Niel here doesn't distract you too much," Kevin said with a grin. Alice headed back up the stairs and packed her clothes into the old backpack she'd been using since secondary school. To her embarrassment, it still had her *A.H* written inside on the label.

"It's been a pleasure to meet you, Julie, Kev. Looking forward to seeing you again soon!"

"Bye Mummy, bye Daddy," Alice said, hugging each in turn, a small tear escaping her eye, as if she wasn't going to see them for a long time. At most, it had been about four weeks in between her visits since she had left home. Alice's parents said their goodbyes, and Alice and Niel left the house, making sure to walk down the path this time rather than the lawn.

Sitting in Niel's car, Alice had memories of her visions from the day before. She was sure it was just a dream, but couldn't help the panic she felt when they approached the road from her dream. Everything was as it always had been though, flowers in place of the vines, no horrible faces on the trees. Alice allowed herself to relax.

"I love this song!" Niel proclaimed, as the car radio blared *A Kind of Magic*. It wasn't one of Alice's favourites, but as Niel sang happily, she couldn't help but join in. Though they had only known each other less than forty-eight hours, Alice was starting to feel that she loved Niel. Everything about him was everything that she had ever wanted. He was a gentleman, he was kind, he'd effortlessly got on with her parents and made a great first impression, he was wonderful in bed, and of course it didn't hurt that it was all wrapped up in a beautiful package. She couldn't tell him this, of course. It was way too soon, she knew, but she couldn't help how she felt for him. Meanwhile, Niel was thinking along the same lines as Alice. She was beautiful, and she didn't even know it, her body, *damn*, she was so sweet and shy, and the way she kissed him made more than just his heart rate rise.

Soon they were back at Alice's building. Walking hand in hand with Niel through the stairwells and corridors, Alice felt none of her normal fear that normally rose up in her chest, step by step. When Alice unlocked the door and they went inside, they heard giggling coming from the kitchen. Rosie, Alice's flatmate, was there with her girlfriend, Laura. They were both only in t-shirts and underwear, and when they saw Niel, each uttered a yelp of embarrassment.

"I'm so sorry ladies," Niel said while turning around to give them their privacy. They ran to Rosie's room to hide from their unexpected male visitor. Their shame didn't seem to last long, as soon after, Alice and Niel could hear giggles coming from Rosie's room.

"Sorry about that," Alice said, hoping that Niel hadn't seen too much of her flatmate and her partner. "They just started going out. I swear Rosie has only become a lesbian to fit in with the rest of the girls in her sports sciences degree. She had a boyfriend two weeks ago."

"Don't worry Alice, I only have eyes for you." He smiled at her. "Well, as much as I don't want to be apart from you, I'd better get back home. Got some stuff to sort out." Alice couldn't hide her disappointment. She'd wanted to spend the rest of the day with him, but, to be fair, they'd been together almost every minute since they'd met.

"We can go for dinner and a drink tonight, if you'd like," he said, sensing her upset.

"OK! Do you know *The Swan*? It's not too bad a pub. Pretty good food." Niel told her that he did indeed know the place, and they agreed to meet at 7pm. Niel kissed Alice goodbye for several minutes, while again touching her chest, until he forced himself to leave, hoping nobody would notice the bulge in his jeans.

"See you soon, beautiful," Niel called as he made his way through the door and out of Alice's sight.

Alice didn't know what to do with herself for the next eight hours. She was bored, frustrated at not being able to have sex with Niel this morning, but she needed to study. She sat down at her tiny desk and tried as hard as she could to concentrate on the chapter about John Bowlby's Theory of Attachment. Nothing was sticking in her mind, however. All she could think about was how much pleasure Niel had given her on their first night together. She could feel herself getting wet and got up from her desk to lie on the bed instead. She totally submerged herself in the memories of that night, the passionate sex that she had had for the first time, and without realising it had slipped her hand into her jeans and experienced another first.

She must have dozed off, as she woke an hour later to the sound of loud music coming from Rosie's room. A little annoyed at being woken up when she still had six and a half hours until she met Niel, she got up and attempted to study again. Now, relieved of sexual tension, she was able to fill the rest of her time exploring Bowlby's fascinating studies of attachment.

The minute-hand on Alice's clock made its round five times until she managed to prise herself away from studying. She stepped into the steamy shower, enjoying the hot water, but disappointed as ever by the miserable water pressure. Once showered, she wrapped a soft towel around her body, not wanting to risk showing anything to the girls in the next room. She spent over half an hour on her hair, blow-drying, brushing, trying to make the most of the natural curls her hair formed. *What should I wear?* She thought. Opening her small wardrobe, the range of clothes in front of her was admittedly pretty poor. All of her clothes were very unassuming, bland even. There were few bright colours, fewer clothes to show her figure. She did have a floral dress that she had worn to a wedding, and noticed lots of the guests, even those with partners, stealing glances at her figure. She spent the next half hour meticulously applying makeup until, at last, she was ready.

This time, without Niel by her side, the corridors felt like they were closing in on her, as if they had a will of their own and the mere presence of Alice was an offence to them. Alice and Niel had planned to meet outside The Swan, but much to her surprise, when she left her building, Niel was standing outside with a bunch of red roses in his hand.

"For you, gorgeous. I spent a long time trying to find a bunch as beautiful as you, but these were the only ones that even came close."

"Thank you so much," she said and stood on her tiptoes to kiss him. The now familiar smell of his *CK Obsession* again causing her to tingle all over. They walked the short journey to the pub, holding hands, blissfully happy in each other's company. The distance would normally have taken them about ten minutes to walk, however they found themselves completely unable to walk more than a hundred steps without stopping to kiss each other. Twenty minutes after leaving, they walked into the warm, cheerful atmosphere of the pub.

"A glass of rosé, please, mate, and a pint. Have one yourself too," Niel told the barman.

"Cheers, mate, very good of you! That your missus you're with?" the short, stocky, and smiling barman asked.

"Certainly is. Punching above my weight or what?"

"Haha, well, I dunno about that, but she's a beauty. You're a lucky man." Niel thanked him and headed back to their table with their drinks.

A couple of drinks later and their food arrived at the table; a burger for Niel and a house salad for Alice. She had wanted the burger, but was fat enough already, so she thought, and couldn't stand the thought of embarrassing herself in front of Niel by spilling grease on her dress. The evening passed too quickly, Alice and Niel so engrossed in one another that they wouldn't have noticed if the barman stripped naked and break danced on the bar. Niel told her so many cheesy jokes, most of them causing a groan and a smile, then a laugh as Niel laughed at his own jokes.

"What do you call a fake noodle?" he'd asked her, already laughing in anticipation of the punchline.

"I don't know," she giggled, "what do you call a fake noodle?"

”An *impasta*!“ he exclaimed, and they both fell into laughter, more caused by the alcohol and their feelings for each other rather than the joke itself.

After a few more drinks, Alice started getting tired, and they made their way out of the pub.

"Do you wanna get a taxi home? You must be freezing," Niel said. Alice was only wearing her dress and a light jacket, but the alcohol was keeping her warm.

"No, let's walk together," she said while linking her arm around his, feeling his strong biceps squeeze against her.

The path they walked was narrow, and they huddled together to avoid walking on either the grassy verge to their left, or the road to their right. The night was dark, the occasional car headlight passing them by, lighting the way more so than the dismal streetlights above them. A car approached from behind, the engine sounding as if it had broken past the red line on its rev counter. Niel turned to see that the car had mounted the pavement and was driving directly towards them. Without thinking, he turned to Alice and shoved her with all his strength into the verge. As he pushed her, he turned just in time to see the driver's face. He was asleep at the wheel. The bonnet of the car made contact with Niel's legs and sent him flying into the air. The first impact he made was with the windscreen. He bounced off as if he were a ragdoll, and flew over the top, then the second, landing with a thud on the road. Alice had managed to stagger to her feet, and in absolute hysterics made her way over to Niel's crumpled body.

"Niel! Niel please! Wake up!" Alice's heart was in her throat, pounding, as her tears fell onto the tarmac.

# CHAPTER EIGHT

B ack in my hotel room, my pain and the sound assaulting me had both ceased. I lay on the floor, my mind clear, coming to terms with the acts that I had committed the night before. Still the memory of the journey from Robert's house to my hotel escaped me. Had I taken another taxi here? If so, surely that will lead back to me. There must be CCTV at the hotel, which would show me leaving in time to have killed Robert and returning post mortem. Terror filled me, weighing down my limbs, as I contemplated the fact that I was now a murderer. I had to plan my next move. Going down for murdering Robert was not going to happen. Especially as he deserved it for fucking Stephanie. He had told me, before I ended his life, that they had only been together twice. Of course, he could have been lying, hoping in vain that his fate was linked to the amount of infidelity rather than the simple act itself. But the look of confusion and sincerity on his blooded face made me doubt what my 'friend' had told me, that it had been going on for a year. And why wouldn't I trust my 'friend'? I had no idea how he had come to know what he knew, but he was right about everything else. I supposed that he must have been a colleague of the late Mr Fields, perhaps a disgruntled underling who had overheard him talking to my wife. Another possibility was that he had wanted a thing with Stephanie too and was jealous that it was Robert who separated Stephanie's legs and our relationship.

Whether it had been two occasions, or a year was, at the moment, a moot point, I decided. Right now, I had to get out of this hotel. I grabbed my dead phone and headed to the door. Down at reception, I handed over my key card, and the receptionist clearly judged the state of my appearance. *That's not good*, I thought. *She's likely to remember me now if she's asked later.*

"Checking out, sir?" she asked, the smile on her pretty face obviously forced.

"Yes, thank you," I managed, Robert's smashed face floating in front of my vision.

"Is everything OK, sir?"

"Fine." I noticed her name tag pinned just above her left breast, and it read *Stephanie*.

"Stephanie?" I asked her, "that's my wife's name".

"Umm, that's nice, sir..." Not understanding her confusion, I looked again at the badge and it now read *Heather*. I had to get out of this place. Without another word, I turned and left the hotel.

Sitting on the Jubilee Line again, my head was filled with ideas, swarming angrily like hornet wasps that had their nest disturbed. I felt sure that people on the tube were staring at me, somehow knowing what I'd done, that I was a murderer. They couldn't know, of course. Paranoia had me in its wicked grasp, escape impossible. How was I to go on living with this huge burden hanging over me, threatening at any moment to snap the last strands of my sanity and crush me? I had to get off the train - the humidity, the smell, the staring faces, it was too much.

Canning Town, the crisp cold air brought me back to reality too suddenly, and I vomited into a drain on the side of the road. Jeering and laughing teenagers passed me by, calling me various vulgar names. I didn't care. They were probably right. Feeling physically unable to walk, I checked my back pocket where I usually kept my bank notes, and found another beaten up £20 note. The wind picked up, my hair already resembled a bird's nest blowing in every direction. I felt underdressed, my ruined shirt providing little protection from the cold. I hailed the next taxi I saw and gave him my address.

"You alright fella?" the driver queried, the second time that morning a stranger had asked, probably concerned about my mental health at least as much as physical.

"Well, I've had a pretty bad couple of days. Step on it, yea?" Suddenly I wanted to be at home desperately and, despite everything, I needed to see Stephanie.

Standing outside the front door, I hesitated before knocking. In my haste to leave yesterday, I'd not taken my keys. I was pondering what to tell Stephanie when she opened it.

"Babe, where the *hell* have you been? I've been so worried about you! Your phone was off and I thought you were hurt or you'd done something stupid or..."

"I've done something stupid. Let's talk inside." We walked through the sitting room where Lily was sleeping sweetly and sat at the dining table.

"Brandon, I'm so sorry about the message you saw. I..."

"I know it was Robert you've been seeing," I interrupted.

"How?" Stephanie was sobbing softly, the guilt she felt for her actions rolling down her face and wetting her plain white t-shirt.

"You won't believe me how I know," I started, and told her about my 'friend' from the park.

"I followed Robert home last night, Stephanie." I was crying now too, as if speaking about the murder out loud made everything real.

"I went into his home. I beat the shit out of him. Stephanie... I... I killed him. He's dead." Stephanie collapsed onto the cold, hard floor.

Lily came running into the room.

"Mummy! Daddy, why is Mummy sleeping on the floor?"

"Mummy is just tired, baby. Why don't you play with your Duplo in the sitting room? Then when mummy is feeling better, she will come and play with you too."

"OK Daddy!" She didn't seem too concerned. Her young mind had no concept of what was happening. I was sitting on the floor with Stephanie's head on my lap when she came to a couple of minutes later.

"Did anyone see you?" Her logical lawyer's mind was whirring, the fact that I had told her I was now a murderer could wait - her priority was making sure I wouldn't get caught.

"I... don't think so. His wife wasn't home. His street was quiet. I don't remember seeing anyone."

"That doesn't mean nobody saw you. Did you touch anything in his house?"

"He came at me with the fire poker. I took it off him, so yea, I touched that." My terror was starting to subside, just being with Stephanie, despite what she had done allowed my heart to relax, my beats per minute dropping below a hundred for the first time that day.

"You didn't leave anything of yours there, did you?"

"I've lost my wallet. I had it in the hotel I went to yesterday. It could be there somewhere... or I might have lost it at Robert's house."

"You fucking idiot. Call the hotel. Ask if anyone has found it. If not, you're going to have to go back to his house. I'm pretty sure he told me that his wife is at a conference this week. If we're lucky, maybe nobody has found him yet."

"Hello, Family First Hotel. How may I assist you?" the cheery voice on the end of the line asked.

"Hi, my name is Brandon Parker. I stayed at your hotel last night, in room 43. I believe I left my wallet there. Could you please check for me?" I asked her, my voice holding the opposite tone to her own.

"Certainly sir. Hold the line." Typical hold music followed and played for at least five minutes.

"Sir?"

"I'm here."

"The cleaners are servicing the rooms at the moment. They didn't find anything in your room, and I've spoken to my colleagues here with me. I'm afraid there's no sign of your wallet. May I take a contact number from you, should it turn up?" I gave her my mobile number and hung up the phone, my hope all but vanished.

"How could you do that to me, Steph?" I asked her, wanting to shift the attention from my own guilt to hers.

"I'm so sorry, Brandon. It only happened twice. The first time was at a conference. We were both so drunk, I couldn't even help myself. And he's so persuasive. He told me, before I saw him the other night, that I didn't really have a choice to go and see him. I'd accidentally let it drop that you'd be away, and he pretty much implied that if I didn't go and see him, I wouldn't be employed much longer." So perhaps my 'friend' was lying about them being together for a year after all. I wasn't sure why, but as both of them offered this towards their defence, I believed them.

"He was blackmailing you?" I asked, and Stephanie sobbed and nodded.

"Steph… I don't really know what to say. This situation is so fucked up. I'm terrified about what I've done. I only remember bits and pieces of it, but I remember taking his life, his blood on my hands, and I remember *enjoying* it. That's what's scaring me the most. I need to forget about the fact that you slept with him for now. I need you, Steph. I don't know how I'm going to get through this, but I know I won't be able to without you by my side."

For the first time since I left the house yesterday, we embraced each other. We held each other and kissed like we hadn't in a long time. Finally, Stephanie pulled away from me, her face displaying the concern and fear that the kissing had masked.

"Not now. Brandon, we've got to go and look for your wallet."

"What if someone has found him, and we turn up at his house? I'll get nicked for sure."

"Let me call his house phone. If there are police or anyone else there, it's likely they'll answer, and it wouldn't seem strange for me to be calling him." My stomach turned. I'm sure it wouldn't seem strange for her to be calling someone she had been fucking.

With each unanswered ring, Stephanie seemed to relax more and more. When the answer machine played the recording of the dead man's voice, she hung up.

"OK. Nobody answered. Let's go."

"No, you're not coming."

"Why the hell not?"

"If the police are there, I don't want you getting dragged into this. You can still claim you knew nothing about any of this." Reluctantly, she agreed. My phone was still dead, so I plugged it into the charger. I looked like shit and thought that if I didn't want to be remembered by anyone who may see me on my way back to the crime scene, I should change into something more appropriate. Robert's street was full of wealthy households, so I changed into a clean pair of smart trousers, a nice salmon pink shirt and a pink and grey striped tie.

"Are you finally going to a job interview?" Stephanie managed to joke despite the deep, consuming fear we both felt.

"You wish."

"Be careful. Make sure if there is anyone outside the house that they don't see you, OK?"

"I will. My phone is dead, so I won't be able to call you. I'll come straight back here whatever happens, OK?"

"OK." We hugged and kissed again, not wanting to break apart. I left the house, again catching sight of my painting of Parliament hanging on the wall, this time feeling love for Stephanie, the gesture of her buying my painting warming me all over, rather than the exacerbating my feelings of betrayal the morning before. I felt confident that nobody would have discovered Robert yet. His wife wasn't home, and as it was a Saturday, he wouldn't be expected at work. Surely this will all work out. I'll go through the door that wouldn't be locked, find my wallet, take the poker with me and bury it somewhere. Nobody will know I was ever there. Except Stephanie and me. The fact that I had murdered someone would forever stain my conscience, but dealing with that can wait for now. Heading to the West Ham tube station, I walked past the park that I'd met my 'friend' in the day before. To my surprise, he was there again, sitting on the same bench. I went to sit next to him.

"Good job, Brandon. You did brilliantly." Again, he was irritatingly talking to me while only looking down at the ground.

"How do you know what I did?"

"Don't worry about that for now. I believe this is yours," he told me and handed me my wallet that I'd left behind. "You left the poker behind too, Brandon. Luckily for you, I've taken care of that for you as well. Nobody will ever find it, trust me. You're going to have to be more careful on the next one though, Brandon," he said through a wicked smile, making eye contact with me once again.

# CHAPTER NINE

## ALICE

Headlights approached Niel's still body and Alice's quivering form that kneeled over him. She stood and walked into the centre of the road, desperate for help. The car pulled over to the side of the road, and an elderly gentleman, in his 70s at least, Alice guessed, struggled out of the car.

"Is everything OK, dear?" he asked, before noticing Niel. The driver that had hit Niel awoke on impact, realising what he had done, and, unbelievably to Alice, driven off without looking back.

"Stay right there. I'm going to call an ambulance." The man, who had previously seemed elderly and frail, moved with surprising speed further down the street and knocked at the door of a large town house. A few seconds later he knocked again, the urgency of the situation sounding into the house through his sharp raps on the heavy wooden door. No answer. He practically ran to the next house, almost falling on the loose gravel underfoot. This time, the occupants answered the door. A young couple, Rebecca and Martin Corrigan, let him inside to use their telephone. Rebecca stayed with the elderly gentleman, who introduced himself to her as Rupert, in the house while he explained to the 999 operator what had happened. Martin made his way out onto the road.

"He's still breathing," Martin reassured Alice after having taken his pulse. There was remarkably little evidence of external damage to Niel. None of his bones were protruding through his skin, though the back of his head was damp with blood from where he struck the road. Alice watched enough drama programmes on TV to know that this was a bad sign.

Alice hardly noticed that Martin had his arm wrapped around her shaking body. She was inconsolable. The man that she had only met forty-eight hours previously but had developed such strong feelings for couldn't leave her alone this soon into their relationship.

"I love you, Niel. Please wake up. These last two days have been the best of my life. Wake up," she begged, over and over. He wouldn't wake up. This was the first time she had told him that she loved him. It should have been under better circumstances. In the distance, Alice could hear the sirens of the approaching ambulance. *Thank God they came so quickly,* she thought to herself. But the sirens soon faded. They were headed to another accident that had happened elsewhere in the city. Niel would have to wait. Alice could almost see the strands of his mortality breaking down in front of her.

Rupert had made his way back to the scene without Alice noticing. He had pulled a pack of cigarettes from his inside jacket pocket and was vigorously smoking his way through his second. He only recently started smoking, which was unusual for a man of his age. The death of his wife had caused him to start. He needed a vice, something to distract him from the pain of losing his wife of forty-five years. Never having been much a drinker, cigarettes became his outlet.

"They'll be here any minute dear," he informed Alice, though secretly, he held no suspicions that they would arrive before Niel left this world. Again, sirens sounded in the distance. Alice allowed herself to hope that this time they were coming for her lover. Soon blue flashing lights carved their way through the darkness, and by the time they had arrived, a small gathering of people stood behind Alice on the pavement, come to gawp at the gory scene to fulfil their basic human curiosity.

Two middle-aged paramedics left the ambulance and approached Alice and Niel. She informed them, as best she could through gasping breaths and endless tears, what had happened. Mark, the larger paramedic with a weak Irish accent, indicating that he'd been in England for some time, removed the stretcher from the back of the ambulance. Very carefully, he and David, the second paramedic, placed the stretcher underneath Niel's still body and moved him into the back of the ambulance with precision. Alice boarded the back of the ambulance without looking back to the strangers who had helped her, or the crowd that was now beginning to disperse, as there was nothing more to see.

"Can you tell me your names?" Mark asked.

"This is Niel Curtis," Alice managed, her grief still uncontainable. "And I'm Alice Hamilton."

"How old is Niel?"

"He's eighteen. Please tell me he's going to be OK."

"I can't promise you anything yet, I'm afraid. We're going to do everything we can for him, but until we get to the hospital, we just can't say."

Before long, the ambulance pulled into Addenbrooke's Accident and Emergency department where Mark and David whisked him away. Alice followed as quickly as she could. With amazing efficiency and care, Niel was soon in a hospital bed, all sorts of machines connected to him. Alice was filled with relief at the sound of the heart rate monitor. The rhythmic beeping confirming his life hadn't yet left him. She stayed as close to him as possible as various doctors and nurses came and went.

"Miss Hamilton? Hi, I'm Doctor Rao," a soft female voice behind Alice explained.

"Hello... how is Niel?" Alice asked, turning to make eye contact with the Doctor. She seemed to be around thirty years old, her dark skin holding onto a youthful complexion. It appeared that the stress and strain of working in the A&E department hadn't yet taken its toll on her.

"Well, it's still early, so I can't say anything for sure yet. This won't be easy to hear, but I can't and won't promise you he will wake up. He has suffered serious head injuries. Even if he does wake up, it's impossible to tell whether or not he has suffered any brain damage."

Alice pondered the possible outcomes and was distraught at the thought of both. Either Niel would never wake up and would eventually die in this hospital bed, or he wakes up a damaged man, his charming personality and wonderful caring nature, gone, replaced by something that even the doctor couldn't predict.

Alice was now alone with Niel. The curtains were closed. His life support was running, the steady beeping now no longer providing Alice with any comfort. She had seen how the car had hit him, how his head had been the first part of his body to make contact with the road, the sickening *crack* sound it had made. She convinced herself that this was it - her relationship with the most perfect man she could imagine, over, almost as quickly as it had started. Despite it only having been two days, she knew she would never recover if Niel died. She had saved herself for a man like him. She knew there was one out there somewhere for her. And now that she had found him, she'd never be the same if she lost him. For the first time in her life, Alice prayed.

*"Dear Lord, I know that I have never prayed to you before, that I've only been to church for weddings and a funeral, but I need you. I'm not a bad person, and I've never done anything bad in my life. Nor has Niel, I'm sure. He is a good man, and I know that he doesn't deserve to die yet. Not here, and not by a hit-and-run driver. I beg you, please, save his life, even if the cost is my own. I would gladly give it to save this man. Please, allow his eyes to open and his personality to remain and I will do anything you ask. Amen."*

She waited. *Beep. Beep. Beep.* There was no sign of movement from Niel still. Suddenly, Alice heard a voice answer her. She looked around, but there was nobody to be seen except for other patients in comatose states.

*"Alice. I can help you. Do you want Niel to wake up?"*

"Of course I do! I'll do anything!" she said aloud in the quiet emergency room.

*"Aaaannnyyyything?"*

"Anything."

*"Well, I was right, it seems. I did tell you that you would need my help with Niel."* The voice from her vision. The voice that spoke to her from everywhere and nowhere, that had no form, but that she could sense all the same.

*"Will you allow me to wake him up? I can't guarantee that everything will be the same as it was before, of course."* The voice spoke through a smile, if the owner of this voice was able to smile.

"Right now, all I care about is that he wakes up. Even if he doesn't care for me, even if he can't remember me, as long as he doesn't die."

*"That's excellent, Alice. He'll soon wake. And Alice, you are in my debt. We'll talk again."*

Alice could still sense his presence, though the voice was no longer speaking to her. She could only describe it as heavy, such a burden, that darkened everything around her. As she looked at the various tubes keeping Niel alive, they slowly transformed into the thick black vines with the razor sharp thorns she had seen before. They pulsed as they pumped their terrible blackness into Niel rather than the various medication and fluids that they should have been providing. Alice could hear the substance passing through the vines, which now appeared to be functioning as veins, as it entered Niel's body. The blackness showed through his skin, all of his veins making their way to his heart like black, writhing snakes. His heart now was visible to Alice, growing darker and darker inside his chest as the gunk being pumped into his body now slowed until it stopped altogether.

The beeping from the heart rate monitor was now frantic. The number on the screen was well over one-hundred and rising with every second. Niel shook violently, back and forth on the bed. His back arched at an almost impossible curvature. Every muscle in his body was tense, and he uttered a deep, guttural groan. His eyes were still closed. Alice screamed and ran.

Dr Rao was walking the corridors in the emergency department, her thick, raven black hair bounced loosely and she seemed relatively unburdened by the eleven hour shift she had so far put in. As she rounded the next corner, Alice came hurtling round and collided with her. Still sitting after her fall, Alice recognised Dr Rao as the person she was hunting.

"Doctor! Please, come quick! Something terrible has happened to Niel!" She climbed to her feet and ran back to Niel's bedside, not helping the doctor to her feet or waiting to see if she was following. Dr Rao picked herself up and followed Alice back to the emergency room, to find Niel in exactly the same state as she had left him previously.

"What's the problem, Miss Hamilton?"

"His veins were all black! I could see them through his skin! His heart rate was really high, and he was almost screaming in agony." Dr Rao found this hard to believe. His beats per minute were still the same as she had recorded onto his medical records previously, and of course, she thought, his veins were not black.

"I understand you're upset, Miss Hamilton. It can be very traumatic to see a loved one in this condition." She dismissed Alice's claims as gently as she could.

"It happened, I swear," Alice told the doctor, obviously despairing over the fact that the doctor didn't believe her.

"Sit down, Miss Hamilton, and I'll go and get you a nice cold sugary drink. It will help take the edge off of your shock."

As soon as Dr Rao left the emergency room, Niel began to twitch. Alice couldn't bear the sight of Niel having the black substance forced into his body again. She covered her eyes and sobbed. The twitching grew and grew until his body was convulsing, shaking the bed. It almost toppling over as it rocked side to side. The groaning again passed his lips, long and deep, until it progressed to a scream. He seemed to have no need to breathe as the scream continued. Alice asked herself why no-one was coming to help. Every artery, every vein and every capillary even had now turned darker than anything Alice had ever seen, as she found herself now unable to look away. Niel sat bolt upright, his eyes still shut fast. The screaming stopped, but still echoing around the hospital. The black retreated slowly, creeping back up his body, until it had vanished.

Niel opened his eyes.

# CHAPTER TEN

## BRANDON

"**W**hat do you mean, *the next one?*" I asked with trepidation.

"Well, you're clearly a natural at this Brandon!" my 'friend' had broken eye contact with me and once again stared down at the floor with an almost scientific interest in the grass below foot.

"A *natural?!* I never meant to kill him."

"Maybe, maybe not. But it's time to start being more honest with yourself, Brandon, and me, too. You enjoyed it. You felt satisfaction as he exhaled his final breath."

My brain felt like it was engaged in a civil war. I couldn't say it out loud. It was too terrifying a thought, but my friend was right. I had enjoyed it, and though I felt dread at getting caught, for some reason, while I was with my friend, that feeling was replaced with something else. The sort of satisfaction that is felt when you know someone has got what they deserve. He fucked my wife after all, and he only regretted getting caught, not the infidelity itself. And who knows how many other women he's slept with? His wife will be distraught when she finds him dead, no doubt. But if she knew the truth about his sordid behaviour, I'm sure she'd feel the same as me. That the bastard deserved it.

"You're right, Brandon. He did deserve it," my friend said, as though he knew what I was thinking.

"Whether I enjoyed it or not doesn't matter," I said, as defiantly as I could, while he still wouldn't meet my gaze. "There isn't going to be a next time, unless you're telling me that he wasn't the only one Stephanie has been screwing around with."

"There are others who need punishment, Brandon. Others who will try to undermine you, judge you, and ultimately, those who will get in the way of our friendship. You wouldn't want that, now, would you? I feel like we're becoming such good friends, after all."

He was right, for some reason that I couldn't fathom, I didn't want anyone to come between us. Whoever he was, and how he had such knowledge of my life, I had no idea. But he was obviously on my side. Not only had he told me who'd been sleeping with my wife, but he made sure I didn't get caught for killing him. I owed him a lot.

"I'll see you soon Brandon", he said to me, upon finally making eye contact. I couldn't explain why, but I was looking forward to it.

When I arrived back home later that morning, Stephanie opened the front door to me before I even took my keys from my pocket.

"Well? Did you find it?" The concern was etched into every crease on her face. She seemed to have aged during the short time I'd been gone. I noticed bags under her eyes that I'd never seen before, her hair seemed lifeless and dull, and her skin was as pale as it had been in the vision I'd had of her the other morning. Not wanting to tell her about my friend, I told her that I had indeed found it on the floor in his house, and that I'd got rid of the fire poker.

"Got rid of it where, exactly?"

"It's probably best that I don't tell you. At least that way, if you're asked anything, you won't be lying when you say you don't know."

"I'm scared, Brandon. Not just of you getting caught, but I'm scared of you. I never thought I'd say that. I never thought you'd hurt a fly, and this morning you tell me you've killed a man. I know I'm partly at fault here, but I can't stay here with you. Lily and I are going back to Mum's." I noticed her suitcase was standing upright in the sitting room, obviously packed for more than a couple of nights away, as the seams were bulging and threatening to split.

"I'll call you every day, I promise. And I will come back home to you. But, you have to promise me something too. You've been frightening me recently. You're not yourself. You've got such a dark look in your eyes. Promise me that you'll go and get help. I've been asking you to for years, but you never have."

It's true, she had been asking me to see a specialist. She knew that I was struggling with mental difficulties, most likely caused by my childhood. I think it was after our fourth date. We'd been out for dinner, Italian as usual. When we got home, we'd made love for hours, and it had been fantastic, one of the best nights of my life, and I'm sure she felt the same way. The next morning, she got a call from her mum. She happily chatted away, enjoying a conversation with her parents as though it's the most normal thing in the world. Of course, for most people it is, but not for me. I'd never known my parents. I know I had spent most of my childhood in care homes, and occasionally for short periods with foster parents, too. A lot of my childhood was a blur, and thankfully so. The few memories I have were not pleasant ones.

"That was my mum!" Stephanie had exclaimed happily on bursting back into the bedroom. "I told her all about us. She said you sound wonderful and that she and dad can't wait to meet you. And I was thinking, I'd like to meet your parents too. Perhaps we could go and see them this weekend?" she asked, her face showing just how keen she was to become a permanent part of my life. I had deliberately not brought up conversations that could lead to us talking about our parents. I didn't want her to know I didn't have any. For some bizarre reason, I was convinced it would change how she feels about me. If she found out I'm not normal, maybe she wouldn't want to be with me anymore.

I told her everything. Might as well get it all out now, I thought. I couldn't lie to her about something as big as this. I told her about the care homes, the abusive staff, the terrible foster parents who obviously were only interested in the government grant, not the wellbeing of the children under their care. She looked more and more horrified as I filled her in on the details.

"Have you ever seen anyone about this? That kind of thing can really cause you psychological problems that you might not even be aware of." I was getting uncomfortable now. I'd never discussed this with anyone else before, and now the only woman I'd ever really had feelings for was telling me I should get help. Why had I told her? I was sure that I'd ruined the relationship now, but Stephanie held me closer, our bodies intertwined, as I silently wept for myself for the first time.

"You need to lie low for a while, too. I'm sure you'll be OK, there's no reason anyone would suspect you for anything, and nobody but you knows that Robert and I were having an affair, so there's no motive for you to have killed him. But I just need to get away for a while. Call me when you're getting help." Stephanie took her case to her car, then came back in and collected Lily.

"Say goodbye to Daddy, Lily. We're going to Grandma's for a little while."

"Can't you come too, Daddy? I want you to come."

"I'm sorry baby, Daddy has a lot to do," I said, doing my best not to let her see me cry. "But I'll see you soon baby. Daddy loves you."

"Love you too, Daddy!" she replied, breaking the dam holding back my tears. I closed the front door and watched from the sitting room window as the car pulled away, not knowing when I would see them next.

The next few days passed in a blur. Takeaway boxes filled the bin and then collected on the work surfaces. I was in no state to cook. I wasn't taking care of myself without Stephanie, I hadn't showered, there didn't seem to be much point. Every time I heard a car outside, I convinced myself that it was the police coming to question me over Robert's death. The curtains hadn't been open in Stephanie's absence, as if anyone did knock at the door, I didn't plan on answering. No knocks ever came, though, and my paranoia proved to be just that. Then came the day of my GP appointment. Apparently, I had to be seen by them before being seen by a mental health specialist. I'd never thought that my childhood had had much of an effect on my adult life, but sitting here, amongst the mess, my bodily odour filling the room, my wife and child gone, and the fact that I may now be a murderer, perhaps meant that I did, in fact, need help.

I managed to wash myself and get dressed, and after standing behind the front door for at least half an hour, finally gathered the courage to face the outside world. The surgery was only a short walk away. After signing in and a short wait, a pretty, short Asian doctor called my name and dragged me away from my thoughts. I glanced at her name badge and realised I wasn't sure how to pronounce her name, Dr Nguyen.

"So, Mr Chapman, how can I help?"

I told her as much as I could remember from my childhood. I could tell this wasn't the first time she'd had someone open up and tell her things that weren't easy to tell. Her facial expression was compassionate and professional, and she listened to me with great care.

"I understand how hard this is for you to talk about. Can you tell me how you think this is affecting you now?"

"Well, my wife has left. Not for good, but she insisted I get help before she comes back."

"And how do you feel in yourself? How would you rate your mood out of ten?"

"One. I have been happy, but lately everything seems to be building up, and I'm remembering things from my childhood that I'd prefer to remain in the past."

"That's perfectly normal, Mr Chapman. Often experiences in childhood such as yours don't cause any problems until adulthood."

We spoke for the next fifteen minutes the questions becoming more and more invasive. Had I ever hurt myself? Did I ever have suicidal thoughts? How was my sexual relationship with my wife? I didn't want to be here anymore. Despite the state of my home, I wanted to be back there. Eventually, Dr Nguyen told me that she would be referring me to a mental health specialist. She could've been referring me to whoever she wanted, I just needed to get home. I felt like I had a giant elastic band around my chest, its rubbery grip tightening with every passing minute. I was covered in a film of sweat, and I couldn't stop my hands from shaking. The doctor told me I'd have an appointment in the next couple of weeks for assessment, and before she'd even finished her sentence, I was out of my chair and into the crisp, cold air.

My head was spinning, thoughts of Robert, of Stephanie, of my childhood, going round and round in my mind like a merry-go-round of anxiety. I managed to pull my phone out of my pocket and compose a text message to Stephanie.

*Hi. Just finished at the GP. Going to be seen by a specialist in a couple of weeks. Come home? I miss you and Lily. Tell her Daddy loves her. And I love you, too.*

I sent it and slipped it back into my pocket. Eager to get home, I zipped up my coat against the cold wind and plodded away from the GP surgery. I barely remember the walk, not realising where I was until I was putting my key in the lock. As I turned it, I felt a terrible feeling of being watched. I was too much of a coward to turn and face whoever it was. Pretending I hadn't noticed, I entered the house as quickly as possible, the smell of rotting left over takeaway swirling into my nostrils. Once in the sitting room, I gathered as much courage as I had remaining and lifted a corner of the curtains. There was someone standing on the other side of the street, looking down at the ground. It was my friend. His face was hidden as again, he wasn't meeting my gaze. For a reason I couldn't explain, for the first time I was scared of my friend. He didn't speak, he didn't move. But I was certain that he wasn't here to help me this time.

# CHAPTER ELEVEN

## ALICE

"Niel! Speak to me!" Alice cried, as Niel looked over at her.

"A...Alice? Where..."

"You're OK, Niel. Everything will be all right now. You were in an accident, but you're in hospital. You're going to be fine." Alice tried to put everything that had happened leading up to Niel opening his eyes out of her mind and allow the immense feeling of happiness and relief take her over.

"I had terrible dreams. It was like I was lost at sea, but instead of being surrounded by water, there was only hatred and terror. Then I heard your voice and somehow managed to escape."

At that moment, Dr Rao came rushing back onto the ward.

"Mr Curtis! I'm very pleased to see you awake so quickly. How do you feel?"

"Confused. Scared, even. But Alice is here with me. I think I'm going to be OK."

Dr Rao performed a series of tests on Niel and eventually confirmed that it seemed he had suffered no brain damage and was very lucky. He had miraculously suffered very little damage, and the wound on his head had already been stitched up. He would be kept in for a couple of nights for surveillance, but providing his condition didn't deteriorate, he'd be sent home. Alice was ecstatic.

"Don't worry, Doctor. I'll take good care of him," Alice promised.

"I'm sure that you will," she replied with a smile. Despite the fact that Niel seemed to be recovering, Alice felt a deep fear spreading through her body. She wasn't sure whether everything that she had seen had been real. How could it be? She wanted to believe it was just another strange vision, perhaps due to the stress of seeing Niel almost die. But she had heard that voice, she knew it, and she'd made a deal with it, without even knowing what it was. Had God answered her prayers? She wanted to believe so. She wanted to believe that not only did he exist, but that He had heard her, He cared about her and Niel, and brought him back from the brink of death. But she didn't. The feeling that accompanied that voice wasn't that of love, compassion, and caring. It felt much more like greed, like opportunism, and, ultimately, like malice. It had told her that Niel may be different to before. Yet here he sat, propped up in his hospital bed, beautiful, with sparkling eyes and a warm, inviting aura.

Alice told Niel everything that had happened, including the kind help he had received from Rupert.

"Strange," Niel managed. "How you kept having visions, or whatever you want to call them, of me getting hurt, and then I did!" That thought hadn't occurred to Alice. Was that just a weird coincidence? She'd never experienced any kind of vision before meeting Niel, so it was hard to believe that it could all be chance. But, if it wasn't coincidence, then it must've been something worse, Alice deduced.

"Well, let's not think about that now. You need your rest." Niel had already fallen back asleep before she finished her sentence.

Alice spent most of her time in the hospital with Niel over the next couple of days. She would rather have been there with him than attending her lectures. After calling the university to let them know why neither of them would be around for the next few days, she' called her friends who were full of sympathy, and offered to come visit Niel in hospital. Politely, she declined, not wanting anyone to see him in this state. The hospital had contacted Niel's parents, who happened to be on holiday in New York. They had planned to cut the holiday short to come back and see him, however, after they had been contacted after Niel woke up, they decided that in the end, it wouldn't be necessary for them to leave America. Alice couldn't believe it. If it was her son, she thought, she'd come to visit him even if she'd been on the moon.

Niel was discharged from hospital on Tuesday morning, having been inside for two nights. Dr Rao had walked over to Niel's bed, a proud smile on her face, and offered Niel her hand to shake.

"Mr Curtis, we're thrilled with how quickly you've recovered. I'm sure she'll take good care of you," she said while grinning a knowing smile at Alice. Niel shook the doctor's hand, and Alice brushed her hair back behind her ear and smiled shily. She couldn't be happier that he was hers to look after. Alice used the phone in the hospital reception to book a taxi back home. Niel was strangely quiet whilst they sat outside waiting for it, but this was to be expected, surely, after he'd experienced such trauma. Alice also noticed that he almost seemed to recoil from her touch. She had tried to take his hand on a couple of occasions, making him flinch, until he stuffed it into his pocket to avoid her trying again.

The taxi journey lasted about twenty minutes, but Alice couldn't help but feel that it lasted a lot longer. Niel didn't speak and gazed out of the window for the entire journey. Alice noticed that the taxi driver continuously stole glances at her in the rear-view mirror, with desire shining in his eyes. She didn't know why, as her reflection in the window horrified her - her hair was a mess, she wasn't wearing any makeup at all, and worse, she had panda eyes as a result of barely sleeping for worrying about Niel.

"Could you stop here please mate?" Niel asked the driver.

"No problem, boss," the driver replied. He stopped quite abruptly on the side of the road, and as soon as the car was stationary, Niel jumped out. Alice was in shock. She had thought that they would go back to her place together, but they were still a couple of minutes away from there. Alice quickly handed the driver £10 and followed Niel out of the car. She could tell he was in a hurry, but his fractured ribs were stopping him from walking very quickly.

"Niel! Wait!" Alice calls after him, her heart in her throat. She didn't understand why he didn't want to talk to her, to touch her. After all, only a couple of days ago, she had told him she loved him. He had been in a coma, but she had hoped that her words had got through to him somehow.

Suddenly, he stopped and turned on the spot, facing her.

"Alice, look, I just want to be on my own, OK? Can you do that for me?"

"Niel, I..."

"Don't. Don't say it. I'll call you, alright? Just give me a bit of time." With that, he continued walking up the street, leaving Alice on her own.

Alice had managed to drag herself to her lectures over the next few days, though she could barely recall anything that her professors had discussed. That was unlike her. She was proud of her studious nature, and never before would she have let anything distract her, least of all a man, but Niel was no ordinary man, she knew. It didn't matter that they had only been together a short time, or that for some of that time, he hadn't even been conscious. She already couldn't picture herself with another man. Niel had had that much of a profound effect on her. Even though he had made no effort to see or talk to her since his release from hospital, she wanted to believe that they would stay together. She needed him. The happiness that he brought her that she didn't know was possible was too young to die.

On Friday evening, Megan and Charlie called round to see Alice, as they had done the previous week. Alice buzzed them up to the flat.

"Ally, what's wrong?" they asked, almost in unison, upon entering her flat and seeing the stress and anxiety written all over her face.

"It's Niel, he..."

"He's OK now, isn't he?" Megan asked, interrupting Alice, as she often does, much to her annoyance. Alice, however, was far too polite to show this to Megan.

"Well, he seems to be. I mean, apart from his arm and his rib. But I... I think he might have left me. I haven't heard from him or seen him since he got discharged from hospital." Alice had been worrying whether or not she would see Niel again, and whether they were in fact no longer a couple, but saying it out loud broke her heart, and she collapsed onto her bed, unable to hold back the tears any longer.

Charlie wrapped her long, slim arms around Alice and held her as she wept. She wanted to be a supportive friend, but she couldn't help but think that maybe Alice was over reacting, at least a little. She had only known Niel for a week, after all.

"Have you not tried calling him at all? Just ask him straight what's going on," Charlie offered.

"I don't know his number," Alice said in between sniffs. "Nor his address."

"Well... y'never know. He did say he needed some time, right? I'm sure he'll come and see you soon. I mean, he's met your parents already, which is mad. I've never introduced a boy to my parents. 'Specially not after only one night together." Charlie laughed, trying to cheer her friend up.

"I really appreciate you girls being here," Alice said. "But..," and she couldn't finish her sentence, her overly polite nature getting the better of her.

"Sure, we'll leave you to it, Ally. But promise you'll come out with us tomorrow night, yea? If you still haven't heard from him, we'll find you a proper man."

"What about you two?" Alice grinned for the first time since she last saw Niel. "You can't always be the bridesmaids, you know."

"Cheeky!" Megan shouted, throwing Alice's pillow at her.

After Megan and Charlie had left, Alice tried to cheer herself up. She went into the kitchen that she shared with six other girls who, luckily she thought, all seemed to be out for the night, and made herself a hot chocolate. She glanced at the dusty clock on the kitchen wall, and despite it only being ten o'clock, she decided to go to bed, the agonising sadness that she had felt at admitting to herself she was single again had worn her out. Before she could get to bed, however, her door buzzed again. Plodding over to the intercom, she assumed it would be Megan and Charlie again. She pressed the button, and recognised the husky, sexy voice coming through the speaker.

"Alice, it's me, Niel. Let me in, would you?"

"Of course!" Alice exclaimed, her excitement building, her past misery a distant memory already. As she was in her pyjamas, she waited for him to come up the stairs, and as soon as he knocked on her door, she threw it open, and threw herself onto him. She took him in in every way possible, the trauma she felt from the three days that she hadn't seen him or heard from him escaped her body as she sighed in relief and contentedness. She breathed in his manly odour, gripped him tight to feel his hard body pressed against hers, and then kissed his perfect lips as passionately as she knew how.

"Where have you been?" she asked, her relief at seeing him now being replaced with anger at how he could disappear on her like that.

"I'm really sorry, baby. Just needed to get my head straight. Everything was going so quick with us. I just needed to slow down. And I don't really know how to explain it, but since I woke up in hospital, I feel... wrong. Angry. And that's not me. I'm normally the most easy-going person in the world, so people tell me anyway. But, like, yesterday I got a call from some telemarketer, and I screamed at them down the phone, like swore my head off at them, and I couldn't help it. I'm getting scared of myself, Alice."

They lay together on the bed, enjoying each other's embrace. As they held each other and kissed, they slowly undressed each other, taking in the sight of each other's naked bodies, as though it had been years, not days. They shared the same unspoken thoughts, of how they were each lucky to be with the other, Niel especially telling himself that she was *way* out of his league. Niel climbed on top of Alice and pushed himself inside of her. Alice gasped and tried to push him back off of her. He was being too forceful. He put his whole weight onto her body, and she was pinned to the bed underneath him as he continued to thrust into her, more forcefully with every movement.

"Niel... you're hurting me..." Alice cried, her voice barely audible, Niel's grunts silencing her protest.

"You like it, don't you?"

"No! Please, can we stop?" Niel didn't stop and put his hand over Alice's mouth. Niel continued to force himself on Alice, despite the tears welling in her eyes and spilling onto the pillowcase. Alice couldn't take it much longer. The pain was unbearable, and she knew she was bleeding down there. Eventually, she felt Niel's body begin to shake as he finished inside her. His hand left her mouth, and instead, to Alice's horror, wrapped around her neck. His grip was strong, constricting her windpipe and sealing it shut. Unable to speak or fight back, Alice stared into Niel's expressionless eyes as her world turned to black.

# CHAPTER TWELVE

## BRANDON

I let go of the curtain and let it fall back into place. For what felt like hours, I sat hunched up against the wall, too afraid to risk another look across the street. The daylight gradually faded into night, and before the dark of night took over, I gathered my courage and climbed to my feet. My knees seemed as if they had been replaced with driftwood, cracking and clicking as I pulled myself up. I gripped the curtains and threw them open. The street was bare, my friend was nowhere in sight. At the same moment, my phone buzzed in my pocket, startling me.

*We miss you too. Lily keeps asking when she can see her daddy. We'll be home on Monday. Mum wants to take us out to a few places tomorrow and Sunday. I got a call from Deborah at work. She told me that Robert is missing. The police found blood at his home, but no sign of a body. We'll talk about it when I'm home.*

No body? I didn't move it. I was pretty sure of that. Well, as sure as I could be. Truthfully, I wasn't even certain that it was me who had killed Robert. The more I thought about it, the more my memories of doing it felt like somebody else's memories. As though, somehow, I'd had visions of his murder. If there was no body, maybe he wasn't even dead? The police had found blood, but how much? That definitely doesn't mean he's dead. I wasn't sure of anything anymore. First the vision of Stephanie having killed Lily, then my encounters with my friend, then the images that came to me in my hotel room, that at the time, felt so real to me. My head was spinning, the room spinning the other direction, my heart in a constant state of palpitation, everything was becoming too much. I couldn't take this uncertainty of my own mind anymore. I needed the sweet oblivion that only alcohol can provide.

After the short journey to the local shop and back, clutching a bottle of Tanqueray to my chest as though it was a prized possession, I poured a double measure over ice, then topped the glass with tonic water. The first sip went down so well, the cold, slightly bitter and sweet liquid starting my journey down a road I knew very well. Each subsequent drink both contained more gin and less tonic. Half a litre of gin later, I staggered up the stairs, barely conscious, and collapsed onto the bed that I miss sharing with my wife.

I woke up to a scream, high pitched, desperate, and felt my heart climb up my throat. Was it in my dreams, or in the house? Too afraid to investigate, I couldn't move from the bed. The house was so quiet that I could hear the beat of my heart echoing around the room. As I lay in bed, I felt a strange presence. That's the only way I can describe it. I couldn't see anyone, but I wasn't alone. The air in the room felt heavy and thick, so much so that it was hard to breathe it in. I was losing my breath and had to get out of the room. Nearly falling over when I got out of bed, I managed to steady myself by leaning against the wall, and slowly edged my way out to the stairs.

Now, standing at the top of the stairs, the feeling of the presence with me in the house was overpowering. It seemed the same as it was that night where I saw Lily's tiny dead body. Despite my fear, I found myself walking down the stairs towards whatever new horror awaited me. At first glance everything looked normal. The house was in the same state I'd left it. The kitchen was a terrible mess, the takeaway boxes still containing scraps of food causing an awful stink. No, that couldn't be the cause of this stench. It swirled menacingly through the air, so powerful that I thought I could even see it. I vomited immediately, luckily managing to get most of it on the linoleum of the kitchen floor rather than the carpet of the living room. There, on my hands and knees, I noticed the true source of the malodour. Stephanie was lying on the floor, mostly concealed by the kitchen units. Her face was the very picture of dread. In the dim light, I could see the white tiles below her were coloured red with the paint of her mortality oozing from large, deep wounds vertically carved into her wrists. Her body was decaying, large pieces of flesh sloughing off her body, her skin almost grey.

This isn't real, I tried to convince myself. Stephanie is at her mother's. Whatever this is, it was the same thing as before. I could almost hear this presence laughing at me, mocking me, enjoying the terror it was causing.

"What do you want from me?!" I screamed into the empty room, less aggressively than I had intended, the wobble in my voice betraying my faux confidence. No response. I sat again with my knees up against my chest, head resting on my knees, eyes closed. I was getting used to this position, it seemed. I couldn't bear to look at Stephanie's corpse lying on the floor, despite being convinced it wasn't real. All of a sudden I heard a whisper directly in my ear, and I could feel the hot, stale breath against my skin.

"Open your eyes."

Against my will, my eyes opened, and I was unable to take my gaze off of Stephanie, my neck locked in place, keeping my tormentor out of view.

"You're quite right. This isn't real, not yet, anyway. I'm showing you your future, her future. You can't deny she has it coming. First she cheats on you, then she abandons you! What a *bitch*!"

"No! I didn't kill her! She doesn't deserve to die. Please..." I tried to beg, not knowing what to ask for first.

The doorbell rang and everything snapped back to reality. The kitchen still smelled. I was still a car crash of emotions, but the voice was gone, the presence had left, and the house felt normal again, and best of all, Stephanie's decayed corpse had vanished. The doorbell rang once again. I got myself together as much as possible, dry my eyes, run my fingers through my hair in an attempt to look at least somewhat sane, and answer the door.

"Brandon, you... look like crap."

"Good to see you too babe," I managed, and kissed her firmly on the lips.

"Daddy!" Lily squealed from Stephanie's arms, and I took her against my chest and breathed in her wonderful smell.

"Hey monster! Did you have fun with Grandma?"

"Yes. We made cakes and cookies and went to the park and fed the ducks and I played on her trampoline and I jumped really, really high, didn't I, Mummy?"

"You sure did!" The sweet innocence of my daughter almost made me forget about everything else that had happened. It was as if her love for me allowed me to build a wall in my mind, though how long until it inevitably came crashing down, I wasn't sure.

I quickly tidied up the state that I had allowed the house to get into in my wife's absence, her reaction at the smell and disorder apparent on her face. Lily and I played with her toys for the next half an hour while Stephanie unpacked upstairs.

"Lily, you wanna watch Cbeebies?" asked Stephanie.

"Yay! Beebies! Daddy, you wanna watch too?"

"Daddy and I need to do something else, but we'll come and watch with you soon, OK?" Lily didn't even seem to hear Stephanie, she was immediately engrossed in Peppa Pig. Stephanie and I went into the kitchen and sat at the dining table, and her face was an unusual mix of relief and concern.

"So the police found Robert. His body had been dumped in a small wooded area near his home. A dog walker discovered him this morning."

"I have no idea how he got there. I swear I'm not even certain I did it, Steph. My head is such a mess." She leant her body up against mine and put her arms around me.

"Well, that's what I wanted to talk to you about. The police have arrested a man for his murder. Apparently, he had CCTV above his front door and inside the house. You were never there. It was Tom Manning, an ex-colleague of mine, that Robert fired for gross misconduct a couple of months ago."

"How... how did he die? Do you know?"

"No, but the official statement was that it was due to a violent altercation in Robert's home, pretty much what you told me you did."

None of this made sense to me. How could I have known how he died without being there myself? My friend had told me that I'd done it, even retrieved my wallet from the scene, told me he'd buried the murder weapon.

"Did the police find a murder weapon?"

"According to the news, he was suffocated to death after being beaten badly."

"That's exactly what I thought I had done to him. This doesn't make any sense."

"No, it doesn't. But let's just be glad that it wasn't you. It must've just been some sort of bad dream. You knew it was him who I... y'know, so it's not surprising you dreamt of killing him. The rest must just be a coincidence", she said, not even sounding sure of her own words. "How did you know it was him, anyway?" I didn't want to tell her about my friend - that would just cause even more uncertainties and problems in our already fractured relationship.

"I was always worried there was something between you," I lied. "And as soon as I knew you'd had an affair, I knew it had to be him. That son of a bitch always wanted you, and I don't think he even tried to hide it, the smug little bastard."

"Are we going to be OK?" Stephanie asked, and when I looked into her beautiful eyes, I knew that we would.

"I think so. I've loved you since you bought my painting, and I still do. It's just going to be hard to, well, be intimate with you for a while."

We spent the rest of the day together as a family once again. I cooked a nice dinner of roast chicken thighs with chorizo and peppers, and Stephanie and I enjoyed a bottle of wine together after Lily had been put to bed. I tried my best to put her affair out of my mind and enjoy her company. Every time she touched me, however, I pictured her touching Robert in the same way, and then I remembered the images of me beating him almost to death, then finishing the job. I think there was a film on in the background, though I had paid it very little attention. The wine was going down well, and I could see Stephanie's face flushing more and more with each glass. Stephanie got up from the settee on her second attempt and went to the kitchen for a second bottle.

Slightly drunk, we went upstairs, Stephanie very unsteady on her feet by then. I helped her into our room and out of her clothes, which she took as a sign that I wanted to make love to her. I didn't. And, even if I did, I doubt I'd be able to get it up, with the weight of everything that has happened recently crushing my libido. She hadn't been too offended at my refusal, and fell into a deep, wine-fuelled sleep. I wasn't so lucky. For hours I lay there wide awake, my thoughts running at a thousand per minute. Just as I was finally on the brink of sleep, the presence returned around every part of my body, locking my joints, making movement impossible. Again, the voice spoke, this time directly into my mind.

"You should enjoy her while you can, Brandon. You've not got long."

Now I recognised the voice. It was my friend.

# CHAPTER THIRTEEN

## ALICE

Alice woke the next morning in agony. Blood stained the sheet between her legs. Her throat still felt as if it was being crushed, and she could barely breathe. But that didn't compare to the pain in her heart. Niel had raped her. It was rape, wasn't it? Of course, she loved Niel, and would willingly sleep with him, but last night she'd tried to get him to stop, and he wouldn't. Had he meant to kill her? She had been warned that he might be different, but when his life was on the line, that was a price she was all too eager to pay. She managed to sit up and get off the bed, wincing at the pain as she struggled over to her make-up table. Her reflection in the mirror displayed the extent of Niel's violence. The shape of his hand could clearly be seen around her neck with a reddish purple bruise. Then a realisation hit her; he could still be in her flat. With caution, she left her room and peered into the corridor. There was no sign of him. The kitchen was the same; empty. It was only 7am, and her roommates would still be sleeping off the alcohol from the night before.

Alice knew she couldn't stay here. Despite the fact that she loved Niel, she was terrified he'd return. She cleaned herself up as well as she could, showering to remove the blood, and put on a high neck top to cover the bruise. She threw some clothes into her backpack and made her way out of the flat. The corridors on the way out of the building never felt more like an enclosure designed to keep her inside. Reaching the stairs, she felt herself drifting away from her consciousness, and realised, before it completely took her in its grasp, that she was having another vision.

She was standing in the same position, the concrete steps descending behind her. Niel was standing no more than ten metres or so in front, his face a storm of anger.

"Don't you dare, you bitch," he called at her. The Alice in the vision felt a sense of escape. She knew she could now be free and this final decision was hers. He'd been in charge up until now, but now she could spite him in one final move and finally win. She felt herself grinning and laughing at Niel manically. Slowly she took a step back, and then another.

"It won't achieve anything," Niel warned her, but she didn't believe him, and didn't care.

"I won't let you do this to anyone else," she said defiantly. She took one more step backwards and fell down the solid steps, colliding with the wall below.

Alice awoke, and was relieved there was nobody else around her. The same steps which, in her vision, she had willingly thrown herself down, now loomed menacingly in front of her. She shuffled along the floor away from them and took the lift. Normally she was frightened of them - she had got stuck in a lift when in a shopping centre with her mother as a child, and that experience still caused her to avoid them whenever she could.

This time, however, the lift was definitely safer, she decided. The thirty seconds or so it took for the lift to reach her floor seemed to take forever, and the journey down to the ground floor must have been even longer. As soon as the doors opened, she threw herself through them, then out of the main doors and into the street. She decided to go to Megan's. She'd let her stay with her until she knew what to do. Alice hoped, at least. Due to her family's wealth, Megan's flat was a little further from the university, but was all her own, no housemates coming home drunk at 3am to disturb her. It was a ten-minute walk away, and for the duration, Alice kept looking over her shoulder in case Niel was following her. Not knowing where he lived worried her. He could come strolling out of any of the buildings around her. She tried to convince herself that she was worrying unnecessarily. Niel had only been good to her before the events of the previous night. Maybe he hadn't meant to hurt her as much as he did. Could the strangling have been part of a sex thing? Megan told her before about a boyfriend she once had who could only climax during sex if he could choke her. Alice had been appalled at the time, but now wished that this is also what Niel had been doing and had taken it too far.

A cool breeze blew across Alice as she walked along the deserted streets. This really was a university city - outside of term time and in the mornings of the weekends there were markedly fewer people lining the high street. Megan's building was on the other side of Cambridge Park, a large, popular green space in the middle of the city. At peak times in the summer the park would be full of sunbathers, picnickers, boisterous boys with footballs and people enjoying small makeshift barbecues. On this morning, it was only Alice, a couple of dog walkers and a smattering of people sleeping rough behind some bushes. As Alice reached the other side of the park, she looked up at the building Megan lived in. There were many signs of the affluence of the residents, the large, heavy oak door with shiny black paint and large gold doorknob, the perfectly maintained balconies overlooking the park, and the lack of grime compared to many buildings in the city. Before Alice could look away, the front door was pushed open, and a man left the building, a man she recognised. It was Niel. Alice wanted to do something, to say something, to scream at him what was he doing there, but she didn't.

Dumbfounded, she watched him walk down the street with his head down and hands in his pockets. She found herself following him as he walked further down the street and got into his brussel-sprout-green VW polo and drive off. Alice wanted to believe that Niel being at Megan's was completely innocent, but her self-destructive mind wouldn't allow her. Her boyfriend and her best friend? This kind of thing only happens in soap operas, doesn't it? Heartbroken, she turned on her heels and headed home.

The corridors of her building almost seemed to revel in Alice's misfortune. The heavy, crushing thoughts were magnified by the creeping darkness. Turning her key into her front door, Alice had never been so glad to be home. She leant against the inside of the front door, catching her breath, realising she hadn't taken a breath whilst walking through her own personal nightmare of the hall corridors. She went into her bedroom and collapsed onto her bed in a state of hysterics, crying and sobbing into her flowery pillowcase. Alice awoke some time later, unaware of how long she had been face down, fully dressed on her bed for. The intercom was ringing. She had no intention of answering it. It would probably be someone for one of her housemates. She herself only had two friends - well, one, now, she thought, and sobbed afresh. She heard one of her housemates padding wobbly down the corridor, presumably also having been woken by the incessant buzzing of the intercom. Several minutes later, there was a knock at her bedroom door. Afraid, Alice gripped onto her duvet and called, "who is it?"

"It's me, Niel. Can I come in, babe? You decent?" Niel said with a chuckle. Fear gripped at Alice, her muscles tense, her body covered in a sheen of perspiration.

"Umm, no. I'm not dressed," Alice lied.

"Ooh, even better!" Niel replied, the happiness audible in his voice. The door opened, and as Niel's eyes met Alice's, shock registered on Niel's face at the state of her own. Her eyes were red and bloodshot, her hair was matted and stuck to the trails of hot tears running down her face.

"Alice... what's wrong?"

"What's wrong?!" Alice almost screamed in reply. "You raped me. You really hurt me. Then this morning I see you leaving Megan's! It was really early, so you must have spent the night with that bitch!"

Alice surprised herself, as she let out all her anger and fear, her words almost taking physical form and striking Niel, the pain of her accusations causing him to almost double over in agony. He sat next to her on the bed.

"You think I raped you? When? I don't understand. I would never hurt you. I... I love you, Alice. I heard you tell me after my accident. I've been too scared by how strongly I feel for you since then to be able to tell you, but I do, I love you too." Alice's cold feelings of anger and fear combined with warm love and relief, causing a tornado of emotion to spin through her.

"I did love you, but what you did to me yesterday, I will never be able to forget it. Look, my neck, look what you did to me. I thought I was going to die."

"I don't understand," Niel said again. "There's nothing wrong with your neck. And I don't know how you can say I raped you. Yea, we did it last night, but you never once told me you didn't want it, and I never hurt you."

"Well, what about the sheets?" Alice asked as she threw the duvet off the bed to show Niel the bloodstain, but was confused to see that it was no longer there.

"What about them? Alice, you're worrying me."

She got up from the bed and looked into her familiar mirror, the only thing that she thought she could still trust. There were no longer any red marks on her neck, no bruising or shadows of Niel's fingers wrapping themselves around her throat. There was no longer any pain between her thighs, and as discreetly as she could, she applied pressure against her underwear with her hand, and again felt no pain.

"I'm sorry if the sex was a bit rough, Alice, but you kept begging me to go harder, so I did. I'll be gentler with you next time, I promise," Niel said, and he opened his arms, inviting Alice into his embrace.

"What about Megan? Why did you stay at her place last night, then?"

"I didn't, I swear. I went there this morning. We were making plans for your birthday."

Alice felt guilt crawling under her skin. Had she totally overreacted to everything? As Niel spoke soothing words to her, she found herself totally unable to believe that he had done anything to hurt her. They embraced each other on Alice's single bed, the whirlwind of Alice's emotion dying down to the warm, gentle breeze of Niel's love. They slept in each other's arms until the early evening, when Niel said he had to go and meet his boys for a night out.

"Why don't you come? I'd love to introduce you to my friends. They'll be so jealous of me," he laughed and smiled his brilliant smile that had repeatedly won Alice over since they had met.

"Maybe next time. I'm really tired. I'm just going to stay here and get an early night." Niel left to go and meet his friends, and Alice contemplated whether she should go and see Megan to confirm Niel's reasoning for being at her place early that morning. The tug of her curiosity and fear of the corridors battled inside Alice's mind until, inevitably, curiosity won. She dressed and tried to make herself somewhat presentable before facing the dreaded corridors and staircases once again. The lift again seemed like the safer option, and at the relief of reaching the ground floor safely, she stepped into the cool night. For the second time that day, Alice was outside of the front door of Megan's building. She had repeatedly pressed the intercom button next to the name plaque that bore her name and several colourful hearts, but no answer came. As she was about to turn and head back home, the door opened as an elderly woman made her way out.

"You trying to get in, dear?" she asked Alice.

"Yes, thank you so much. I forgot my keys." Alice surprised herself with the ease of the lie. Alice had been here several times before and climbed the stairs to the third floor. There was no fear or heavy, pressing panic in these corridors, until Alice reached Megan's apartment, and saw that the door was slightly open. Alice pushed the door all the way open, and immediately felt the same dark, gripping horror that was now so familiar to her from her corridor.

"Megan? It's Alice. Where are you?" Alice asked from the doorway, too afraid to go inside. There was silence in the flat. She slowly padded through the hallway, the soft carpet giving way beneath her feet.

"Megan, I'm scared." As she walked further through the hallway, the dark fear almost guided her into Megan's room, the heavy atmosphere tugging her towards what she knew she would not want to see. Tentatively, Alice pushed Megan's bedroom door open. Megan's feet were at eye level to Alice, slightly twisting back and forth. A thick rope hung from the chandelier on the ceiling, the other end wrapped around Megan's neck.

# CHAPTER FOURTEEN

## BRANDON

A few days had passed since I had last heard from the figure I used to call my friend. Now I wasn't sure what to call him. 'The figure' will do for now. Life was passing by in a grey blur, my emotions neither happy nor sad. I constantly felt as though there was a fog between my eyes and my brain, blocking most of my conscious thoughts. I refused to allow myself to think about what the figure had last said to me. To enjoy my wife while I could. That I haven't got long left with her. Was he threatening me? I couldn't be sure. Perhaps he again knew something that he couldn't possibly know. Maybe Stephanie was going to leave me? I wouldn't blame her, I suppose. I've hardly been a good husband. My recent mental state was undoubtedly pushing her further away from me, as her deceit and betrayal was pushing me. Robert's death has visibly affected her as well, exacerbated by the uncertainty as to whether it was me or this Manning bloke that killed him. It felt like we simply co-existed, rather than living together. After putting Lily to bed one evening, Stephanie approached me with the words that often cause panic in a man's heart – we need to talk.

"About what?" I asked with feigned ignorance.

"Don't pretend that everything is OK, Brandon." She used my entire first name. It must've been serious. "We're hardly talking, we're not happy, and it's starting to affect Lily. She just asked me why Mummy and Daddy were sad all the time. And you've been drinking a lot again. That's not a road you should be walking again." I looked down into my fourth empty glass of gin and tonic and decided that she was right.

"Well, what are you proposing? You going to find someone else to sleep with?" I asked, regretting it immediately.

"No, that's never going to happen again. But I can't be here for a while. I need to try and get my head around everything. Luckily, I've got my work conference in Edinburgh this week. I've asked Mum to look after Lily for the week. Use that time to sort yourself out. Do whatever you need to do, but when I get back, I want to be your wife again rather than whatever the hell we are to each other right now." I'd totally forgotten she had that conference, if she had told me in the first place.

"OK. I'm going to work while you're away, then. This will be my last stab at success with my painting. If nothing comes of it – well, I'll finally bite the bullet and start looking for a proper job." Stephanie's stress visibly lifted at my promise of looking for a job. As much as she loved my artwork, she was a realist, and knew that the chances of me ever becoming successful were a lot slimmer than I'd become recently. I blamed my ever-increasing gut on stress, but I don't think that the endless takeaways that I ate for lunch and solo dinners helped either.

I'd always been stick thin as a child. Living in the care system does that to you. I didn't even know food could be enjoyable until I was an adult. Growing up without parents was, in my own opinion the cause for most of my problems. Not being successful – well, that must be because I didn't have a role model. Difficulties with forming relationships – that must be due to the years of being bullied at school and at home. I liked to believe I was a good father to Lily, but if I ever did anything wrong, well – that must be, because I had very few positive role models growing up, countable on one hand, no knowledge of what a good parent is. On the few, short occasions where I had foster parents, they were far from good to me. There was Mr and Mrs Berrington, the first couple that adopted me. Rich, respected and privileged, they had everything except the ability to produce their own offspring. When I refused to suck his dick and bit it whilst he tried to make me, that was it, back in the familiar yet dreaded orphanage.

Then there was Mr and Mrs Kennedy. It was obvious they only took in foster kids for the payments from the government. The money that was provided for the foster children instead primarily went on drugs, injected into their veins rather than filling our bellies. I was so hungry while living with them that I stole £10 from Mrs Kennedy's purse to get food for Sally and Becky, the other foster children, and myself. She caught us tucking into chocolate and bread in Becky's room. I took full responsibility and ended up back in the orphanage again. At least they fed us, shit though it was.

Monday morning came around, the weekend again a grey blur, most of it spent in front of the TV, mindless rubbish thickening the fog in my brain. Stephanie kissed me goodbye, and for the first time in days, I enjoyed physical contact with her. I held her in my arms. Her perfume filled my nostrils, and there was a stirring in my trousers, something which hadn't happened since I'd learnt of her betrayal. Lily came running and jumped into my arms, her beauty and innocence slightly lifting the fog.

"Imma miss you, Daddy. Can't you come to Grandma's too?"

"I wish I could, honey, but Daddy has a lot of work to do. I'll come and pick you up at the end of the week though, OK? Then we can have cake together and watch Cbeebies."

"Yay! I love you, Daddy!" Lily exclaimed, and tears of happiness formed in my eyes at my love for her.

After Stephanie and Lily had left, I felt the fog returning.

The days passed slowly. For the first two days, the only productive thing I had done was to order ten new canvases and some new acrylics. My familiar diet returned, as did the stack of empty takeaway boxes piled up in the kitchen. I can cook, and enjoy it sometimes, but there never seems to be any point that I'm only cooking for myself. I was acutely aware that this wasn't going to be improving my attractiveness to my wife, however.

When I awoke on Wednesday morning, I swore that I would be more productive, that I'd eat more healthily, that I'd work out. After a light breakfast of orange juice and Marmite on toast, I set up my easel and painted. I made very little conscious effort in my work, and just let the brush guide my hand across the canvas. When I finally stopped and looked at my work, I had painted what seemed to be myself on the night that I had seen Lily's dead body, and Stephanie in her terrifying, nightmarish form. I was sitting against the corner, my arms across my knees, my head down. The only colour on the canvas was a deep, royal blue, tears collecting on the ground below me. Dark swirling patterns covered the rest of the surface, taking the form of a man standing in the background, watching over me. He wore non-descript clothes and had no face. I recognised him, despite his lack of features, as the figure I had formerly called my friend. Had he been there that night? Had the rest of the horrific events blinded me to his presence?

Tired from the stress of recalling memories of that night, I ordered yet another takeaway, my usual of a half-pound burger, chips and chicken wings. The man on the other end of the phone didn't even ask my address. How depressing is that? He recognised my voice and order. It must be time to stop now. I didn't want to end up like that woman I'd read about in the news. She ordered pizza every single day until the day she died. She had no family or friends, and the only reason she was discovered dead was because she didn't make an order one day, and the concerned delivery boy went to check on her. Despite my guilt and concern for my own wellbeing, I was eagerly awaiting my delivery. When the food arrived, I handed over £15 and told him to keep the change. I didn't hear a reply through his motorbike helmet.

I took my food to the kitchen and poured myself a large glass of wine. I opened the bag and was greeted by the familiar smell of grease and hot polystyrene, and my stomach gurgled in anticipation. I dropped myself into the groove my ever expanding behind was carving in the settee and flicked on the television. My favourite comedy series, *Peep Show,* was on, and my mood lifted as I laughed and drank wine. I brought the heavy burger to my mouth and took a large bite. A thick, slightly liquid substance filled my mouth, and I vomited immediately. I examined the burger in my hand, and instead of the meat patties, a black substance oozed from between the bun. In my horror, I threw it across the room. The substance seeped out of the burger and into the container, and I felt an inexplicable fear from looking at it. I ran to the kitchen sink and spat into the sink. More of the black substance lay amongst the piled-up plates and mugs. I turned on the tap to the maximum, and, too afraid to touch it or look at it, I left it running before backing out of the kitchen. I gathered up the burger container and the rest of the food and threw it into the wheelie bin outside. The horror and the evil I felt from the substance stayed with me the rest of the evening and invaded my usual nightmares of my childhood that night. I had several dreams that I could've sworn were real. In them,

I was lying in bed, alone, with the dark evil sludge dripping from the ceiling, heavier and heavier, landing on my face, drowning me with its evil presence.

The next morning, thankfully, the wheelie bins had been emptied, allowing me some respite from the dark invasive thoughts from the night before. After forcing down my breakfast of four Weetabix, my mobile phone rang for the first time since Stephanie had gone to her conference. I assumed it would be her calling to check on me, but the screen on my mobile told me otherwise. It was Steve Foster.

"Brandon! How you doing? I've not heard from you for a while, mate."

"Steve. Yea, not too bad, I guess. You?"

"Ooh, that bad, huh? What's up?"

"It's nothing, honestly. Just struggling with my work. I haven't really painted anything that I was proud of for a while now."

"Come on, mate, your work is always amazing. I bet you've got a stack of canvases there that are much better than you give yourself credit for. And that's kinda why I'm calling. Got an exhibit coming up in a couple of days. Wanna be there? Got a bigger space for you this time."

"I don't know."

"Come on, it'd be good for you to get your name out there. I'm sure you could sell a few pieces. I'm not being entirely selfless here, either. I could do with some good commission," Steve said with a laugh.

"Alright, I'll come. But I can't promise you'll make much money off of me," I told him honestly. Steve gave me the details, and we said our goodbyes.

I forced myself to sit in front of the easel again and get some work done. I finished two paintings that day. The first was of the London skyline with a sun setting behind it. Not my normal kind of work, but

I was very pleased with the beauty of it and had a confidence that I didn't normally feel that it would sell. The second I have no memory of painting. The setting was a bedroom. An ornate wooden four-poster bed took centre stage. The rest of the room the detail was slightly blurred, as if out of focus. A naked woman was on the bed, her hands handcuffed to the bed behind her. There was a man straddling on her, plunging a red handled knife into her chest. Her mouth was wide open in pain and horror, the realisation of her own mortality in her eyes. Looking closely, I realised the man was me, and the woman someone I did not recognise.

"Good work, Brandon," the figure said from behind me. "Great minds really do think alike."

# Chapter Fifteen

## Alice

It took Alice a while to realise that the scream was coming from her own mouth. She dropped her handbag and fell on her behind, onto the floor. Her feet scrabbled for purchase against the wooden flooring, and she backed herself into a corner. Megan's eyes were bloated, staring down to the floor, her final moments of horror snapshotted on their green irises. Alice screamed and sobbed, until without realising, a man had entered Megan's flat and was taking Alice away from the horrors of the bedroom.

"Hey, are you OK? What's your name? I already called the police when I heard you screaming. They should be here any minute. What happened?"

"I don't know... she... she's my best friend," Alice managed to utter through sobs.

"What's your name?" he repeated.

"Alice. Alice White."

"OK, Alice. I'm Ben Davis. I live two doors down. What happened?"

"I found her. She... she can't be dead." Ben offered Alice his embrace, and Alice took it gladly. She sobbed into his shoulder until the police arrived. They escorted both Ben and Alice from Megan's apartment, and Ben offered his own apartment as somewhere they could discuss what happened. He opened the door for them and allowed Alice and two police officers into his home.

"DCI Waters," the tall, blonde officer said. "And this is Detective Jarvis." She nodded at the shorter, heavier, balding officer beside her. Ben offered his and Alice's name to the officers and informed them of Megan's name.

"So, which one of you found, Miss Hayes?" asked Waters.

"That would be Alice here," Ben informed them. "I heard her screaming and went to see what was going on."

"Is that correct, Miss White?"

"Y... yes. She's my best friend. I came to see her and found her hanging from the ceiling."

"How did you get in?"

"She didn't answer the intercom. But an old lady was leaving and opened the door for me. Then when I got up here, Megan's door was open," Alice told the officer, her voice shaking.

"I see. And did you see anyone else apart from the lady that let you into the building?"

"No. There was nobody else." Jarvis remained silent, eyeing both Alice and Ben with a suspicious gaze.

"How do you both know Miss Hayes?" asked Waters, her tone remaining passive, with a slight hint of commiseration.

"She's my classmate at uni," Alice said.

"I don't know her at all, though I have crossed paths with her in the building a couple of times," Ben added.

"Do you have any reason to believe that she would have wanted to take her own life?" Jarvis asked, speaking for the first time. Alice's devastation renewed at his questioning, and lack of remorse in his voice.

"No. Not at all. She was always so happy. She had everything to live for."

"Did she have a boyfriend that you are aware of?" Jarvis asked.

"No."

"And can I ask where you have been yourself today, Miss White?"

"Well, I was actually here this morning. I came over to see her as I was upset with my boyfriend, and then I saw him leaving her building, so I went back home." Alice regretted telling him this immediately.

"Your boyfriend was here? At what time?"

"I suppose it was around 8am when I saw him leave."

"What's his name?"

"Niel. Niel Curtis."

"And what was his purpose for being here?"

"He told me that he was planning my birthday party with Megan. At first, I obviously thought maybe something was going on, seeing him leave her place so early, but I believe him."

"We will need to speak to him. Can you please provide us with his contact details?"

"I actually don't know where he lives, or his telephone number," Alice said, embarrassed. Jarvis gave her a look of slight disbelief.

"In that case, please ask him to contact us as soon as he can. It's very important." Alice gave the officers her address and telephone number, and they told her they would be in touch. Crime scene investigators had arrived at Megan's home and were collecting evidence. Alice was not allowed back in to collect her handbag, instead one of the officers handed it over to her. Not knowing what else to do, Alice said goodbye to Ben and left the building.

As she stepped outside, the wind hit her as hard as her sorrow at losing her best friend. The police obviously believe that Niel may have had something to do with Megan's death. Alice wasn't sure what to think. Was there any way that he could have been involved? Alice tried to consider this objectively. Megan was hanging from the chandelier, but due to the exuberance of her home, the ceilings were very high, and Alice couldn't imagine how she would've been able to hang herself at such a height. She didn't remember seeing a ladder or anything like that, though she wasn't sure she'd be able to remember anything other than the image of her friend's face of horror and death, which would undoubtedly be branded into vision. Alice couldn't recall having told Niel when her birthday was, which was coming up the next weekend. But of course, Megan could have told him, and asked him to come around to make plans. Niel had seemed genuine when explaining why he had been at her apartment. She needed to see Niel.

Alice arrived back home fifteen minutes later, her gait slow as she tried to imagine how life would be now without her best friend. She was so concerned with her own thoughts of Megan and Niel that the corridors barely registered with her as she approached her front door. She went inside and ignored the group of girls giggling and laughing in the kitchen. She unlocked her own door and saw Niel sitting on her bed.

"Hey Alice!" Niel said with a grin. He didn't know about Megan yet then. Alice managed to tell him, her grief almost bubbling over into hysteria. His attempts to calm her by stroking her hair and rubbing her back had no effect.

"How was Megan when you saw her this morning?" Alice asked.

"What do you mean? Do I think she was going to kill herself? No, of course not. She seemed fine."

"Well, there must have been a reason she did it, if she actually did kill herself, which I don't really believe. The police want to talk to you. You may have been the last person to see her alive."

"I'll call them now," Niel told her.

"I need your address and phone number," Alice demanded. "I don't know why you haven't given it to me already."

"OK, sure. I haven't been hiding that from you, you know. I just fell for you so hard that I've been happy to be the one to come and see you rather than getting you to come to mine. Also, my housemates aren't particularly nice people, so I'd rather visit you," Niel said, hearing the accusation in Alice's voice. Niel made his call to the police and spoke to Detective Waters. Due to it being late evening, he agreed to attend the police station for an interview the following morning. This calmed Alice somewhat, as she felt that they weren't assuming his involvement already.

Niel visited Alice again the next afternoon. The police had questioned him thoroughly, regarding the reason for his visit to Megan, their relationship, whether they were having an affair. They told him they would need to speak to him again in the future, but for the time being Megan's death was not being treated as suspicious, despite Alice's protest that she would not have killed herself. Over the next couple of weeks, Alice tried her best to attend lectures at university as normal. Megan's funeral had been held, during which Alice met Megan's parents for the first time. Over a hundred people packed the small church on the outskirts of the city. Several of her lecturers from the university attended, along with many students. She had been well liked by her peers, but, like Alice, kept herself to small groups of friends. Charlie was present as well, her and Alice supporting each other as best they could, both finding it difficult to talk about Megan in the past tense.

Since Megan's death, Niel had been Alice's rock. He seemed to be at Alice's apartment more often than her housemates. Sex with him since the time she thought she had been raped had been nerve-wracking to begin with. She had even been hesitant for him to see her naked. She was convinced by now though that she had dramatised the whole situation. Why would Niel have raped her? She wasn't sure whether it was a real or imagined memory that she kept telling Niel to go harder, but the love and affection he showed her constantly eroded her belief in the rape and blamed herself for thinking Niel could be capable of something like that. As their relationship developed, they frequently skipped the protection before having sex, as Niel told Alice that he could barely feel anything when he used a condom.

It had been three weeks since Alice had met Niel in the student union bar, and, much to Alice's concern, and at her best guess, more than six weeks since she had had her last period. Not wanting to worry Niel with her it, she walked into town one morning after Niel had left to go to a lecture and bought herself a double pack of pregnancy tests. Once back home with the tests, she convinced herself she was worrying over nothing, and put the tests back into her drawer and the worry to the back of her mind.

Niel came over to visit again that night. He and Alice lay together on her small bed, her head resting on his muscular chest.

"Do you have any plans this weekend?" he asked her.

"Yea, I was going to go back to my mum's, actually. I haven't seen her since we went together, and it'd be good to talk to her about... everything," Alice replied, still finding it hard to talk about Megan's death.

"Oh." Niel said with disappointment in his voice. "I was hoping we could maybe go to a hotel together or something. Get away from this city, spend some time in a bed that's wider than I am for once. Try some different positions." He grinned.

"I'm sorry. I've already told Mum I'll be going; she'd be upset if I cancelled on her now. Your idea sounds nice, though. Let's do it next weekend?"

"No, fuck that. If you would rather be with your mum than me, fine. I understand." There was anger in Niel's voice.

"What? No, it's not like that at all. It's just I told her first."

"Yea, fine. You go and see your bitch of a mother." Niel dressed quickly and left Alice alone, despite her protests and her begging him to stay.

This wasn't the first time that Niel had exhibited an outburst like this, but Alice was worried that they were getting more frequent. Was this still a result of whatever change that the voice she heard promised? She had been able to put thoughts of what had happened that day to the back of her mind, to lock them behind a door, but they were breaking out. As the horror of Niel's accident and the subsequent things she had seen overwhelmed her, Alice felt her consciousness slipping away.

Alice again had the same vision as she had had a few weeks previously. She was at the top of the stairs, backing closer and closer to the top step. Niel came running at her, telling her to stop, but it was too late. She was tumbling, rolling down the stairs, crashing into each concrete step. As her head collided with the wall, she woke back on her bed. Managing to overcome her fears, she again locked the door in her mind, keeping them at bay, though for how long she couldn't be sure. Her visions, Niel's behaviour and Megan's death would one day have to be dealt with, she was sure. Today wasn't that day. She knew if that door opened again, she would drown in her own emotion. Instead, she opened her drawer, removed the pregnancy test, and went to the bathroom.

# CHAPTER SIXTEEN

## BRANDON

As soon as I turned around, the figure was nowhere to be seen. When I looked back at my canvas, the same black substance that had been in my food was smeared all over the canvas. Despite the foreboding the blackness caused in me, I couldn't tear my gaze away. It seemed to move across the paper, gathering in one big mass in the centre of the canvas, with black trails leading up to it. Each streak of black seemed to have a pulse, pumping the nightmarish liquid across the surface into the bulging heart in the centre. With a fresh burst of confidence, I ran across the kitchen and grabbed the largest knife I could find. I gripped the wooden handle with both hands, and with as much strength as I could gather, I drove the long steel blade through the writhing, beating black heart. I pulled the knife back out of the canvas. The wound that I had caused it simply healed over, the pulse growing faster and angrier. I dropped the knife to the floor in horror and dismay, narrowly missing my foot. I grabbed my newly opened bottle of gin from the kitchen cabinet and gingerly took the canvas from the frame. The French doors in the kitchen were open, and I threw the painting onto the patio outside. I upturned and emptied the contents of the bottle, and once the painting was thoroughly doused with alcohol, I lit a cook's match and threw it into the abhorrent blackness. It immediately caught fire, and burned satisfyingly, thick dark smoke rising to the heavens. I watched the painting burn until neither canvas nor black substance remained.

I went back in the house and found more wine. The cool liquid soothed my throat, which had been burning from inhaling smoke. The first bottle went down in no time, and I staggered to the fridge for another. I craved the sweet release of oblivion that only alcohol can provide. As I sat in the dark sitting room, drinking, alone, I contemplated how my life had got into such a state. My marriage was failing. Not only because of the deceit of my wife, but how I'd been towards her. Not only have I been letting her work all the hours under the sun, and many under the moon, while I sat at home failing to forge a career as an artist, but I've not been giving her anything to come home to. A fattening, depressed husband after a difficult day at work is far from what she deserves, and I understand how I drove her into the bed of another man. I don't deserve her. She should be happy, and it's evident that she's not. We have been, of course. We used to make each other laugh and satisfy each other in bed, but it's been several months since either of those desires have been sated.

My mobile phone rang, and Steve's friendly voiced boomed into my ear.

"Brandon, mate. Not heard from you. You are still coming down to the exhibition today?"

"Shit, sorry, totally forgot." I panicked. Leaving the house frightened me. Everything frightened me recently. I was beginning to doubt my own sanity. The things that I've been seeing haven't been real. The only explanation that I allow myself to consider is that everything that has happened is due to stress, any other explanation would involve acknowledging the supernatural, and to hold on to the remaining threads of my sane mind these are thoughts that I could not entertain. The thought of having to go somewhere and interact with people wasn't pleasing to me, but I seriously needed to make some sales on my art, to make Stephanie proud of me, and to make smalls steps towards improving our relationship. Make her happy again, make sure that she doesn't have another affair. I couldn't cope with that feeling a second time.

"Brandon? You there?"

"Yeah, sorry. I'll be there. Remind me when and where."

"Come on, Brandon. Your memory is getting terrible in your old age", Steve teased. "Doors open at 6pm, so get there an hour or two before that and get yourself set up. It's in the Elizabeth Exhibition centre in South Bank."

"I know it. I'll be there."

I picked six of the canvases that I was most proud of, including the painting of me sat in the corner with the figure watching me. I hated the picture, and wanted rid of it, so if someone would buy it, great. I realised that I hadn't showered since Stephanie had left, a bad habit of mine. I turned the shower on, and felt immediate relief when getting under the hot, powerful water. My anxiety for the evening ahead and the fear of everything that had happened recently flowed down the plughole. After showering and drying myself off, I tried to give Stephanie a call. It went straight to her voicemail. Thankfully, her own voice spoke to me down the line, rather than the voice that I had heard previously. I decided not to leave a message and got myself dressed in some smart jeans and a striped shirt. With a few hours until I needed to leave, I sat on the sofa and tried my best to clear my mind, to mentally prepare myself for social interaction. I pulled my phone out of my pocket, and to my surprise, found a packet of cigarettes. I had totally forgotten I had bought them several days past whilst drunk. I hadn't smoked for years. Recent stressors must have caused me to relapse – though, the pack had not yet been opened. As I pulled the packet out, a pack of matches I must have bought at the same time fell out. It dropped just underneath the sofa. In my laziness, I let it lie there.

The day passed in a relative blur in front of the TV until it was time to leave for the exhibition. The district line of the London Underground took me all the way to my stop, Embankment, where I walked the short journey to the exhibition centre, carrying my heavy canvas holder. I had been here before and honestly had never imagined I'd be able to display my work here. I owed Steve a lot for getting me in here, and I hadn't really shown him any gratitude yet. I would have to take him for a drink if any of my pieces sold. I went through the main entrance, and there he was, the picture of confidence. He was wearing a white suit, and his ginger hair and beard were meticulously groomed to perfection. His personality was very flamboyant. He didn't care what people think of him and refused to listen to ridicule for either his hair or his homosexuality. And that's partly why I respect him so much. He has had a hard life but has overcome all his difficulties and stands proud as the victor. The complete opposite of me.

"Brandon! Great to see you, mate. Especially so much of you!" He laughed and poked me in the gut.

"Ha, yea, I know, I've put on a bit of weight. Catching you up," I replied.

"Oi oi, less of that, you cheeky bugger. Come on, let me show you where you can set up." Steve led me through the hall, packed with artists all displaying work much more beautiful or provocative than my own. My position in the hall wasn't the best, by far, but I couldn't begrudge Steve that. I shouldn't even really be here, let alone in a good spot. Nevertheless, I got my pieces set up on their easels, and took my seat. Before long, the hall started filling up with a variety of people, a couple of small-time journalists, many art students donning a diverse array of hats, and rich people looking to cover their house with work from artists most people have never heard of in an attempt at feigning culture. I shouldn't think this way about them, but most people that come to these things have no understanding of art.

Throughout the evening, a smattering of people walked past my stand, glancing over my work with no more than a passing interest. One woman wearing a beret and a long flowing flowery dress told her husband that she thought my London skyline painting would like nice in their sitting room, but her husband in a tweed suit turned his nose up and they walked on.

A couple of hours later and I managed to sell a large painting I had finished a few months previously of Stephanie's face in a beautiful black and white profile, tears rolling down her face. The woman who had bought it said she could feel the raw emotion in the painting and couldn't resist buying it. I felt a pang of pride that I had managed to portray Stephanie's beauty in paint. I sat back in my chair, content for the evening, and drifted off into a light doze. When I awoke, there was a man standing and starting intently at my painting of me in the corner of Lily's room. He was angled away from me, and the high collar of his shirt and the rim of his hat hid much of his face from me.

"That's exactly how I remember it," he said.

"I'm... I'm sorry?" I stammered back.

"Well, I was there, remember?" The figure wasn't looking at me. A familiar fear spread through my nervous system, my skin crawling.

"You. What do you want from me?!" I asked, my voice quivering and weak.

"Nothing, Brandon. You're doing great as it is. First that prick Fields, then that useless whore in her own bed. I gotta say, Brandon, I really admired your work on that one. Inspired. I honestly can't wait for the next one."

"Listen to me, you bastard," I managed, without conviction. "I didn't kill Robert. That was one of his employees, it's on CCTV. And who is this woman you're talking about?"

"You painted it just like it happened, Brandon. How could you know how she died if you didn't do it yourself?"

"You're insane! I didn't kill her, just like I didn't kill Robert."

"Then how do you remember killing him? How did you leave your wallet there that I had to pick up for you? And you might wanna read the evening newspapers, Brandon. She is dead, and you killed her. You should be proud of yourself! I knew you could do it!" The figure still wasn't revealing his face to me, and I couldn't take not seeing him any longer. I grabbed his shoulder and immediately felt the familiar pain of hundreds of needles piercing my skin. I yelped in pain and staggered backwards, knocking over my easels. Again, there was no visible mark on my hand, but the pain was so real. It seemed to course through the rest of my body, my hair standing on end and skin turning deathly pale.

"Don't be like this, Brandon. I really think we could become the best of friends if you'd just let it happen. I could even be a father figure to you! It's not like you ever had much of one in your sorry life."

"You're insane," I repeated, struggling for words. "You know nothing about me."

"Don't disappoint me, Brandon. I'll see you soon. Think about what I said. It's in your own interest." He turned and left the hall, and I was rooted in place, unable to follow him.

Once he was out of sight, I gathered my courage, able to move again, and ran out of the hall as fast as I could. I didn't care about taking my artwork or payment from Steve. I needed to get home. I wasn't sure that I'd be safe anywhere, but I couldn't be outside any longer. I ran into the tube station and touched my Oyster card on the gate for the district line. The journey back home was long. I could feel other passengers staring at me and silently judging me. I was quite visibly a wreck of a man. I arrived at my stop and climbed the stairs out of the station, my heart heavy, my legs more so, each step a monumental effort. I stopped by the local newsagents, and my heart stopped as I saw the advertising for the local evening newspaper. The headline read *Local woman brutally murdered in own home*.

# CHAPTER SEVENTEEN

## ALICE

A strange and unusual calm descended over Alice as the pregnancy test revealed her fate. Moving without thinking, Alice padded down the hallway into her bathroom. She turned on the shower, the lukewarm water dribbling into the bathtub. Alice peeled off her clothes, only now realising how much she had been sweating. Naked and shivering, she sat in the tub and wept.

Alice had always known that she would love to have a child one day. Her mother had been an inspiration to her, always putting Alice first over her own needs. But she had also always wanted to go to university to study psychology. Alice was fully aware that she had had a privileged childhood and wanted to one day become a clinical psychologist to help those who hadn't. Now both of her life's wishes were happening at once. She was pregnant while at university. Her mind tore straight down the middle. She could visualise both futures, the family life with Niel and their baby, and her own successful career, but no baby in sight. She allowed herself to wallow in the depths of her own thoughts while the shower continued to trickle over her blonde hair and down the curves of her body, unaware of time passing.

Fresh truckloads of anxiety dumped their loads at Alice's feet as she considered how she would tell Niel, and more so, what his reaction would be. He had been having increasingly aggressive outbursts recently; the tether holding his anger at bay snapping at the slightest tug. Alice had been afraid to even cross words with him, and she was terrified that her pregnancy would be the catalyst that would bring their short, but intense relationship to a fiery end. They had only been together a few weeks, and were both so young to bring up children, let alone having little money – though Niel had mentioned the inheritance he'd received, Alice had no idea how much that was. She couldn't put this off, though. Niel had to know that she was carrying his baby. She picked herself up, dried and put on her soft cotton pyjamas.

Back in her room, Alice drank a glass of water and attempted to swallow down her dread with it. She picked up her phone and called Niel. He answered on the second ring.

"Hey, Alice, what is it? I was just about to go to sleep," Niel said with a deliberate yawn.

"Umm, well, I, uhh, have something kind of important to tell you. But I'd rather see you and tell you in person. Can you come over in the morning?"

"I guess. I'm going to go and play football with the guys at 10, but I'll come over before that, at like 9 o'clock. It better be important," Niel said, hanging up, not waiting for Alice's response.

Sleep didn't come easily for Alice that night. Every time she was on the brink of falling into unconsciousness, her roommates would wake her by laughing like a pack of hyenas or throwing another empty bottle into the recycling bin. When sleep finally came, harrowing images forced their way into her dreams. She was lying in a dark and unfamiliar place, with Niel stand beside her, rubbing his hands ecstatically. She was in labour but was not pushing the baby out of her–instead; it was clawing its way out of her womb, bursting through her skin with an excruciating, demonic scream.

Alice awoke to find, to her dismay, that in the horror of her night terrors, she had wet herself. She angrily tore off the sheets and left her room to put them in the communal washing machine. To her relief, her housemates all appeared to have gone to bed, or, more likely, had passed out in the living room. She filled the machine with powder and fabric softener and went back to bed to lie on her bare mattress. There she lay, curled up facing the wall, her back against the darkness and her fears, until finally morning arrived.

Niel arrived promptly at 9 o'clock, as he said he would. After letting him in to the flat, Alice couldn't help but notice that his good looks were no longer as prominent and eye-catching as they had been when they had met. His looks weren't the reason she loved him, of course, but the look on her face now filled her with concern and anxious anticipation rather than lust. His smile, instead of lighting up the room, now seemed sinister, the corners of his lips turning into a maniacal grin. His eyes were dark and deep pools of venom, the sparking, inviting brightness that had first attracted her now but a memory. Alice wanted to believe that she was either imagining these changes, or that they were a result of his accident he had been involved in. But if she allowed herself to accept what she truly believed, it wasn't either of those. It was the voice that had spoken to her on the night of the accident where all hopes of Niel surviving had left her. She had heard a voice offering her Niel's life, at a cost, which she had taken without consideration. And now the bailiff was claiming what was owed.

"So? What is so important?" Niel demanded. Alice couldn't speak, unable to swallow her trepidation. She opened her bedside drawer and handed him the pregnancy test. Niel's grin widened, and for the first time in days she heard him laugh. A melodic, genuine laugh. He was happy.

"Alice, I don't know what to say. You're really pregnant?"

"Yes. I've been afraid to tell you. I didn't know how you would react," Alice said, while searching Niel's face for signs of him taking the news in a less than positive manner.

"That's..." a grin spread over Niel's face, "excellent. I've always wanted offspring. A child, I mean."

"So, I mean, you're happy? You want to actually have a baby together? We're both so young, and we're still studying. How are we going to afford it, or have time for it?" Niel's face darkened once more, then anger and hatred almost appearing to cloud his eyes with darkness.

"You're surely not suggesting that we get rid of it, are you?"

"I don't know. I don't know what to do. I was up all night trying to decide what we should do. We both have plans for our lives - plans that don't include us having a baby just yet. I've never really thought I would consider an abortion, but we're not ready, and I'd never want to give birth to a baby and put it into care."

"Alice, we will have this baby. Everything else is just details that we can worry about later. I want this."

"I don't know. I suppose mummy would help us look after it during the week."

"No." Niel cut Alice off mid-sentence. "No, we'll have this baby, and we'll look after it. It's just you and me now. I don't want anyone else involved. Don't even tell your mum. It's none of her business. Anyway, I've got to go to football. Maybe see you at the weekend?" Niel kissed the top of Alice's head and left before she could protest.

Despite the fact that Niel had seemed pleased by the news of the pregnancy, Alice was becoming increasingly concerned with the fickleness of his behaviour. She had no ability to predict his reactions or his actions towards her. Why wouldn't she want her to tell her mother about the pregnancy? Alice herself was slightly worried to tell her, as her mother would no doubt worry about her future at university and the career that Alice longed for, but there was no doubt in her mind that Julie would support her completely in whatever she chose to do. Both her mother and Niel had got along very well, so what was Niel's problem?

Alice sat alone on her bed, her chin resting on her knees, and drove her mind in continuous circles of thoughts between Niel and the pregnancy. Thoughts of what she had potentially agreed to, in order to save Niel's life, continuously permeated her thoughts, intruding on her fragile mind. Finally, allowing herself to consider the ramifications of what she had done, she wept. She wept in horror at what she had seen, what she had heard, and what Niel was slowly becoming. What were the motivations of whomever the voice belonged to? Why had it chosen Niel, and what did it want from them both? She had never felt a fear like this in her fairly sheltered life. The dread pumped through her body, her heart tight in her chest, her limbs shaking, and her fingers full of pins and needles. The sensation filled her organs, and her body reacted violently, as Alice reached urgently for the bin beside her desk and emptied the contents of her stomach into it. Her greatest angst throughout her life had been not knowing what was going to happen in any situation. She spent countless hours considering what the possible outcomes of any difficult situation could be, gradually working herself into a whirlwind of anxiety until she finally managed to convince herself of a positive outcome. She knew that generally the worrying was worse than any outcome, but this situation with

Niel and the voice she had bargained with was unprecedented, and this time she was unable to even find a positive outcome, let alone convince herself of the chances of it coming to fruition. She couldn't bear feeling this way anymore. She had to get away. She picked up her phone and called her mother.

Julie answered on the ninth ring until which Alice had become convinced that something had happened to her mother.

"Hello?" Julie answered, and Alice already felt some of her apprehension leave her body.

"Mummy. It's me."

"Hello love, how are you? Everything OK?"

"Umm, I... not really, Mummy. I'm not feeling well. Can I come and stay with you for a few days?"

"Of course. You know you're always welcome. But what about your classes?"

"It'll be OK. It doesn't matter if I miss a couple of days. I'm too ill to go in anyway."

"OK, well, I don't want you getting on the bus while you're ill. I'll come and pick you up. Your father is out playing golf for a couple of days, anyway. See you in an hour!"

Alice started to feel slightly better, the calming effect that her mother always had on her, allowing her mind a moment's respite. She forced herself from her bed and packed her bag with clothes for a few days and headed for the kitchen to fix herself some lunch. On opening her bedroom door, her nostrils were assaulted by the smells of her flatmates' night of inebriation. Vodka, leftover takeaway food, and the acidic aroma of vomit caused her to recoil in disgust and lose her appetite. Alice wasn't aware, but she was rapidly losing weight. Her ribs were protruding from her body, the bony ridges visible under her clothes, and her figure was losing some of its former concavity. She had never been anything of a glutton, and her already small appetite had almost vanished since Niel's accident. Some of her beauty had left her face, dark rings had formed under her eyes, her cheekbones were more prominent, and her skin had a grey quality to it, reflecting her increasingly listless disposition.

Eventually, Alice's intercom rang, and she rushed to answer it.

"Hello love, I'm downstairs." Julie's voice rang through, crafting the first smile in some time onto Alice's face.

"Be right down," she replied.

As Alice closed the door to her flat behind her, the apprehension for seeing her mother was instantly forgotten as she once again faced the dark, shadowy and foreboding staircase. She tried to gather what little strength she had left in her reserves and face the stairs with rationality and confidence, but this deserted her with each stride she took towards the stairs. Once she reached the top step, her body was covered in a sheen of sticky sweat, her fingers were carving crescent moons into her soft palms, and she had to deliberately control her bladder else let it empty where she stood. She felt a presence behind her, and could almost see Niel standing behind her, his face wrought into an expression of hatred and, strangely, concern. He wasn't there, and she knew he wasn't, but she could see him all the same. Calling on her final reserves of energy, she unclenched her fist, gripped the bannister bolted into the concrete wall, and took her first steps towards the ground floor. The shadows awaiting her in the corners appeared to reach out to her with dark, pulsing tendrils, eager to entwine her in their horrific embrace. Running now, Alice eluded their grasp, and eventually reached the front door. Despite how hard she pushed, she couldn't get out. Her conscious mind had now all but abandoned her in her state of catatonic fear, as the tendrils from the stairway snaked silently towards her, ever pulsing, ever oozing their horrific innards onto the ground below. Finally, Alice remembered that she needed to pull the door, not push, and burst out into the sunlight and a cool wind. The sudden contrast from the hot, overwhelming fear of the corridor to the frigid wind outdoors shocked Alice, along with the malnourished state of her body, and her knees surrendered to the pull of the earth.

# Chapter Eighteen

## Brandon

I struggled to open my eyes. When had I closed them? Light poured forth through the fraction that they were open. White tiles on the ceiling. My eyelids surrendered and retreated, meeting each other and sticking together with the mucus that had somehow built up. I fought to open them again, feeling as though I was battling against slipping into unconsciousness. I was exhausted, and the temptation to allow sleep to claim me was almost overwhelming. My eyes opened just enough to part my eyelashes, and a tall, thin construct loomed over me, a bag hanging from it. My eyes closed. Opened once more. The bag was full of a black substance. Darkness as my eyes closed again against my own wishes. Once they opened again, and the blurriness passed, I was aware of a figure in the room with me. I could not move in time to see them as my eyes succumbed to the need to close again. This time, I was unable to force them open.

"Steph?" I think I asked out loud, though couldn't be sure whether the thought passed my lips or merely echoed in my thoughts. Where was I? The smell, the light, the small part of my surroundings I had managed to glimpse reminded me of hospital. Why? Wasn't I just at the art exhibit? I couldn't remember leaving. I didn't want to be there. Hospitals frighten me at the best of times, and this certainly wasn't one of those. Still, at least if Steph is here, I began to think, then realised, shit, it can't be her. She's in Edinburgh, and I can't have been here long enough for her to have made that journey. A realisation gushed through me, clotting in my veins – it was *the* figure here with me.

Footsteps, slow, deliberate, approached me, and stopped to my right. I could feel the figure lean over me, their hot, rancid breath against my neck, raising goose bumps down my entire body.

"You're *weak*, Brandon," the voice rasped directly into my ear. "You're far too weak for what you need to do next. But don't worry. I'm making you *strong*. Soon you'll not only do what needs to be done, you'll *want* to do it." The putrid breath no longer hung in the air and the presence I felt from the figure, gone. My eyes snapped open, I sat bolt upright in bed, and I screamed.

"Brandon! You're awake. My god, are you OK?" I was suddenly aware of my surroundings in the hospital room, and of Stephanie standing beside my bed to the right, gripping my hand tight enough to leave nail marks behind. I looked at the drip bag, now containing its usual clear liquid rather than the black mess.

"Where is he?" I demanded of Stephanie.

"Who? The doctor? I'll get him for you. Are you OK? How do you feel?"

"Not the doctor." I ignored her questions. "That damned man. I don't know who he is, or what he wants from me."

"What man? What are you talking about? Lie down, Brandon. I'll get the doctor." Stephanie clearly hadn't seen him. But he had been there. I knew it. He was real. I lay down again, exhausted. The next thing I became aware of, Stephanie was beside me once again, with a stern-looking man next to her.

"Mr Chapman. How are you feeling?"

"I, I don't know. What happened to me? Why am I here? And how long have I been here?"

"What's the last thing you remember?"

"Well, I was at an art exhibit, then nothing. I woke up here."

"You've been here for about thirty-two hours, Mr Chapman. We believe you lost consciousness from alcohol consumption. We have pumped your stomach, and we're now hydrating you. Tell me, how much alcohol have you been drinking recently?" I looked at Stephanie. She looked at me, a pleading in her eyes, and I knew I had to tell the truth.

"Rather a lot, I suppose. I've been very... stressed recently."

"Can you define a lot for me, please?"

"The better half of a bottle of gin a day," I admitted with shame.

"Well I can say with almost 100% certainty that that is why you are here. Your wife also mentioned that you have been suffering with delusions, that you believe that there is some kind of figure stalking you." It's not delusions, I know it's not. But why try to get this doctor to believe me? No. The easiest thing to do was to go along with it being due to the alcohol.

"I've just been drinking too much. I'm not delusional or schizo-phrenic or anything like that," I replied, whilst the doctor eyed me with suspicion.

"We're going to keep you in another night for surveillance and hydration," the doctor informed me sternly, before moving on to his next patient.

On our way back home the next day, Stephanie collected Lily from her mother and I had never been more glad to see her. Stephanie refused to return to work and booked a week off work due to a family emergency. She told me that she was not only ashamed of me, but terrified that, if left on my own, I'd drink myself to death. I understood her concerns completely, and also doubted that if I was left alone, that I would wake up from the next self-abuse of my body via alcohol. Looking into Lily's innocent, loving face, I couldn't face the idea of leaving her without a father and was suddenly struck by the knowledge of my own mortality. I had to stop behaving so selfishly. How did I expect to be able to rebuild my marriage like this? Things were bad enough with Stephanie having cheated on me, but surprisingly, that no longer caused me distress. The weight of my other stressors – the figure, my visions, the deaths of two people weighed the scales so heavily that my other problems were lifted out of reach.

When we arrived back home, I had an overwhelming desire to be as close to Lily as I could. Every moment felt precious. Lily, like most children her age, had a passion for almost everything shown on Cbeebies, the kids' TV channel. Peppa Pig was her absolute favourite, and when she wasn't watching it, she was playing with her Peppa Pig toys, or having me tell her stories in the voice of Daddy Pig. The afternoon passed all too quickly, whilst I remained in a constant state of bliss and love for my daughter, allowing myself to forget recent events as much as possible. I was vaguely aware of Stephanie tidying up the vast mess that I had created in the few days while she was away. Any guilt that I felt from letting her clean on her own was soon forgotten by the warm, innocent love of Lily as she lay on my lap, hugged me, kissed me. Stephanie cooked a light, healthy dinner, clearly concerned by my ever-increasing waistline. We ate together as a family, and though both Steph and I engaged in conversation with Lily, the atmosphere between Steph and me was markedly less positive. Soon it was time for Lily to go to bed. She insisted that I be the one to take her, and that I tell her Peppa Pig stories. I spent a wonderful fifteen minutes by her bed side, before she fell asleep with a beautiful smile on her face. I kissed her forehead and took one last look at her before closing the door behind me.

"Brandon," Steph said to me on my return downstairs. "I'm very worried about you. I'm sorry again for the things that have happened between us recently but, to be honest, I don't think that excuses your recent behaviour. And this man you say you've been telling me about, I'm really concerned that you're seeing things. The alternative, well, it's hard to believe."

"I've been seeing him a lot more recently. And other things besides. They certainly seem real."

"What sort of things?" I told her about the visions of her dead body, mangled and rotting, of the terrible black substance, everything that had happened to me recently. I was more aware now of the background noise of the TV.

"Patricia Harris, a retired social worker, was found brutally murdered in her own bed this morning by her daughter. Police are asking for anyone who was in the area and saw anything suspicious to come forward." A map was shown on the screen, indicating the rough location of the crime. "Mrs Harris, a retired care worker, formerly ran the South East London Children's Home, and lived with her widower husband, Chris Harris. Her family have been informed of the tragedy and are asking for the press to respect their privacy during this difficult time."

"Christ!" I shouted at the TV. "Fuck me! That was Mrs Harris? My God."

"What?" Stephanie asked, shaken by my outburst. "You know her?"

"Shit, yea. That's the children's home I used to live in. She was a wicked bitch. Never touched me, but I swear she got off on making us kids feel like shit. She always belittled us, degraded us in front of the other kids, and used to scare me shitless. But fuck, I can't believe she's dead. I painted the exact picture of her death, and I swear, just like Robert, I feel like I did it."

I was aware of the female reporter speaking again. "Police believe the murder was committed with the victim's own kitchen knife. The weapon was missing from a distinctive set of knives with coloured handles and would have looked similar to the knife on screen," she said, as an image of the knife with the red handle that I painted in my picture, and saw in my own hands, was on display.

"I saw that knife. What the hell is going on?" I begged, my voice quivering and weak as I shook and wept.

"You didn't kill her, Brandon. You're just convincing yourself that you did, and for some reason, you're subconsciously thinking that you remember details that you can't possibly know. I don't know what's happening, but we'll figure it out, I promise," Stephanie said, whilst gripping me tightly in a much-needed embrace. "You should tell me more about what happened when you were young. I'm sure if you talk about it, things will gradually get better."

"You know I don't remember much. I had a pretty bad time in that care home, and with a certain foster family, but nothing that would fuck me up this badly."

"Tomorrow, let's call the South East London children's home and request your records. Maybe there will be something there that you can take with you when you have your psychologist's appointment. We will get to the bottom of this I promise," Steph kissed me. Despite everything, I felt her kiss arouse me. Steph switched off the TV, and sat astride me, her hands on the back of my head, and she kissed me, long and hard. It felt good to lose myself in the kiss, to leave everything behind and allow myself to completely give in to the pleasure of her touch. It had been so long since we were even this intimate with each other. Feeling the obviousness of my physical arousal press against her, Stephanie took me by the hand and let me up the stairs to our bedroom. I lay down on the bed, and she resumed her previous position, sitting upright on my lap. Stephanie gripped the hem of her shirt and pulled it over her head. I fawned over the sight of her figure, the shadows cast by her curvaceous form, the slight bounce of her breasts as she removed her bra and threw it across the room. She then reached down, undid my trousers, and slipped me out of my trousers, wasting no time in slipping me inside her. She rode me as if we were horny teenagers, not a married couple with a young child. I was enthralled by her shape, her hair flowing as she bounced on top of me, my hands on her hips helping her up and down, until I could no longer contain myself and exploded inside of her. The release was exquisite, and Stephanie clearly felt the same way as she climbed off of me and collapsed into the bed, her head resting on my chest.

"I love you," she said, breathing heavily

"I love you too," I replied, a smile on my face as I allowed myself to believe that the worst of my problems were behind me.

Several hours later I awoke, the night still shrouding the house in darkness, save for the light from the streetlamps filling the room with dim light through the open curtains. I desperately needed the bathroom. Throwing on my dressing gown, I stepped into the hallway. Silence. I padded down the corridor and paused outside Lily's bedroom. Not being able to help myself, I opened her door slightly and leant against the jamb. In the pale light from her nightlight, I could see her small chest rising and falling in a beautiful, reassuring rhythm. I gently closed the door and entered the bathroom. The cool tiles felt good against my feet. I lifted the toilet seat and began to urinate, as I heard a scream from our bedroom. The shock of the awful sound tearing through the silent night gave me such a fright that I jerked, missed the toilet bowl, and covered the floor in urine. Stopping immediately, I ran down the corridor to our room. The door wouldn't open.

"Stephanie!" I screamed and was only met with the same scream I had heard from within the bathroom, muffled this time. I pounded on the door, punched, kicked, barged as hard as I could. Eventually, the frame shattered, and I collapsed into the room. I wanted to not believe that what I was seeing was real. It couldn't be, along with everything else that I had seen recently. My doubt in no way lessened the fear caused by the scene in front of me. There was a smell that carried through the air, along with the horrific sight. A smell of iron, of sulphur, of rot. There were awful sounds, wet, writhing, pulsing. Our marital bed with the beautiful white cotton sheets was crawling with thick, black tendrils, almost as thick as my arm. They sprouted from underneath the bed, writhed and twisted around Stephanie's pale skin. Almost her entire body was covered with these abhorrent, intertwined entities. Suddenly, a voice. From everywhere and nowhere. Inside my head and outside. Dark, deep and echoing, yet familiar. The figure. Though I couldn't see him, I knew it was him.

"This doesn't have to come to happen, Brandon. Not like this. Soon, though, we'll be together again. Think of all the fun we can have!" With that, he was gone, along with the tendrils. Stephanie was fast asleep in bed, as though nothing had happened. The thought of seeing the figure again, despite what he had just shown me, filled me with an uncomfortable feeling of anticipation. I couldn't explain the hold he had over me, but I wanted to see him again, to know what he was planning for us to do next.

# CHAPTER NINETEEN

## ALICE

Julie moved with surprising speed to catch Alice as she collapsed. One hand around her waist, and the other under her arm, she walked her carefully to her car, parked in the parking bay ten metres away.

"What on earth is wrong with you, Alice? You look awful. Do you need to go to hospital?" Julie asked.

"No, Mummy, I don't want to go to hospital. I'll be OK."

"You're covered in sweat! And you're stick thin. Have you been eating? Let's get you home and give you a good hot meal." Growing up, whenever Alice had felt unwell, that had been her mother's solution to everything. A good hot meal. And she always provided. She wasn't a professional chef, would never win Masterchef, but she cooked with such love and passion that Alice felt the food not only in her stomach but warming her heart as well.

"Mummy, before we go anywhere, I need to tell you something," Alice managed to say, with her head bowed, her once beautiful hair now hanging lank and dull over her face. "I'm pregnant."

"Oh, Alice. How do you feel about that? Are you happy?"

"Do I look happy?" Alice snapped, out of character. "I could've been. But, when I told Niel, he was so weird about it, like he has been about everything recently. He even told me not to tell you I was pregnant."

"Did he now? Well, we'll talk about him later. How do you feel, though? Do you want a baby?"

"I don't know. I never thought I would even consider abortion until now, but... I'm not ready to have a baby. I don't even think I can take care of myself properly, let alone a baby. And I love Niel, I do, but he's been so different. I don't think it's a good idea."

"OK, love, no need to work yourself up over it now. But no wonder you're not feeling well. I was as sick as a dog when I was pregnant with you, even after only a couple of weeks. You really need to eat something, get your strength up, especially as you're eating for two. Come on, let's get you home and fed."

Alice began to feel slightly better in the familiar comfort of her family home. She sat in her father's armchair. Kevin allowed nobody but his little Alice to sit in his chair. The chair had been moulded over years by Kevin's rather large behind, but she felt comfortable and safe there. Before long, she fell into a disturbed, haunted sleep. She dreamed she was falling, but she did not wake due to the sensation as she normally did. Instead, she went further into her nightmare. Now she was in an unfamiliar and uncomfortable bed. She tried to get up, but could not, her wrists bound to the frame. The last sight she saw before waking up, sweating and shivering, was again of Niel tearing the baby out of her, laughing, howling, shrouded in intense, wicked joy.

Alice awoke to the smell of bacon, toast, beans, and sausages. Julie had prepared her one of her famous fry-ups, which were more than partly to blame for Kevin's pot belly, as Julie affectionately calls it. Growing up at home, Alice had been treated to the breakfast every weekend, despite the fact that she spent most of the time pushing the food around her plate rather than into her mouth. The grease that collected at the bottom of the plate did nothing to encourage her appetite, but once she started eating, she realised how hungry she really was. How long had it been since she'd eaten a proper meal? She had no idea. Minutes later, the plate was clean, and Alice relaxed back into her chair, and drifted off once again, this time, much to her relief, into a deep sleep without nightmares.

Once Alice awoke in the early evening, feeling more well rested than she had in weeks, Julie came and sat on the arm of her chair and wrapped her arm around Alice's shoulder, warming her in the embrace that only a loving mother can give.

"So, tell me, sugar lump, what's been going on with you and Niel?" Julie asked, the concern etched into the fine wrinkles around her bright eyes.

"He's... been different ever since he was hit by that car. Sometimes he can be so loving and caring, but that seems to be happening less and less... and more often, he's not..."

"Has he hit you?"

"I... yes. I probably deserved it, I guess. He wouldn't have done it if I didn't." Julie gripped Alice's face and pulled her gaze up to meet her own.

"Cut that out right now. There's never any excuse for a man to hit his partner. Especially not you. You've never done anything to upset anyone. I didn't raise you to say stupid things like that."

"Sorry, Mummy. But I think I might have done something. That day he got hit by a car... I prayed, I prayed and prayed for Niel to wake up. The doctors didn't think he would ever wake up again. But my prayers were answered. Some...thing spoke back to me. They told me they could save Niel, for a price, and I accepted... I didn't ask what the price would be. I was so selfish. I just did it."

"Can you hear yourself, Alice? You can't really think you did this? That something spoke to you and made Niel wake up? Stress does things to your mind, makes you think things that never happened did, and vice versa. You'd just seen the man you love almost killed, and you think you're going to be in complete control?" Alice couldn't deny that her mother's words made sense, and she wanted, so badly wanted to think that her recent experiences could be attributed to something so simple as the flaws of the human mind, but she knew this not to be the case. She knew that arguing this with her mother wouldn't get her anywhere. Not that Julie didn't care about what Alice was going through, quite the opposite, but she was the kind of person who believed the evidence of their own eyes over the testament of another's tongue, even that of her daughter.

"So what are you going to do about Niel? If you want to know what I think, and even if you don't, I'm going to tell you, anyway. Any man that hits a woman is no man. I'm sure he apologised and told you that it'll never happen again. He's convincing himself, not you. I really liked him when I first met him, and, well, I guess I'm not as good a judge of character as I've always thought I am. I want you to leave him, Alice. I'm not having him hurt you again."

"I don't know Mummy. I can't decide right now. I've got bigger decisions to make."

"You know I've never agreed with the idea of abortion, it's always seemed like a cruel thing to do, but if you decide you don't want to have a baby with a man who hurts you, I'm right behind you, sugar lump. Whatever you decide to do, I'm with you a hundred percent. But there's no need to decide what you want to do right now. There's plenty of time for you to make up your mind." Alice knew, however, that the decision was made. Being apart from Niel, and back in the loving environment of her family home made her realise that, were this child to be born, it would never have the same childhood that she felt so blessed to have had herself. How could she raise a child with a man who was cruel to her? The child, no doubt, would eventually come to understand its father's behaviour, and resent not only his weakness but her own in not doing anything about it. With a newfound determination, her mind was set. She was not going to continue her pregnancy. When she was going to have a child, it would be on her terms, when she knew she could give it the life it deserved. She would tell Niel first, hopefully while at her mother's place in case he reacted badly, then she'd give him an ultimatum. Change his behaviour, no excuses, no empty promises, or she would leave him.

She called Niel. He picked up after the second ring.

"Alice, where are you? I've been trying to call you."

"I'm at my mothers. I..."

"You told her. I thought I made myself clear."

"Yea, well, she's my mother. Anyway, can you come here? We really need to talk."

"I'll be there alright. And you might want to reconsider – we will be having this baby." He hung up. Shaken, Alice went back downstairs. She joined her mother in the living room, and Julie opened a bottle of wine, poured herself a large glass. Despite the decision she came to, she didn't think it appropriate to join her mother for a glass. They sat together, Alice making small talk to avoid discussing the pregnancy or Niel any further. The evening passed gradually, the hours on the clock above the fireplace passing as the bottle of wine emptied.

Julie kissed Alice goodnight, and unsteadily, due in part to the wine and partly due to her arthritic knee, made her way up the stairs to bed.

Not wanting to be on her own, Alice headed up to the bathroom, and stood in front of the mirror. Having never realised her own beauty, the physical changes of her face and body were hardly noticeable to her own eye. She brushed her teeth, for almost ten minutes, as she usually did, a bad habit that she could admit to but could not stop. She spat into the bowl and was horrified to see that the toothpaste had turned a bright red colour, a metallic taste overpowering the minty toothpaste. She opened her mouth wide and looked into the mirror, and gasped as she caught her own gaze. Her eyes were pure white, no iris visible, and dark veins branched from her corneas down her entire face, pulsing and beating with the rapid rhythm of her heart. Alice let out a gasp and backed away from the mirror, but her reflection did not move, instead mocked her with a maniacal grin.

Against the wall of the bathroom, Alice slowly dropped to the floor, crying hysterically. Her vision slowly brightened. Everywhere she looked took on a white quality, brighter and brighter until she could see nothing but white. Deep, rasping voices came at her from all angles. Mocking, insulting, cutting her with their rancour and vitriol. She covered her ears with her hands, but the voices reached her mind, regardless. She suddenly became aware of a crushing presence, the very atmosphere seeming to be her enemy, pressing, triturating her spirit, grinding her strength. Thunderous roars and crashes echoed through her brain, robbing her of another of her senses. Blind, and deaf to any other sound, she crawled, slowly, deliberately, towards the bathroom door. She had to get to her mother. The door was closed, and from her position, practically parallel to the floor, she could not reach the handle. The weight of the presence would not allow her even to rise to her knees, such was the power and the weight of its force. The floor beneath her shook, pounded in time with the deafening cacophony in her head. She felt a liquid oozing from her ears, her eyes, her nose, and once more a metallic taste flooded her mouth.

Silence. Silence so sudden, Alice's ears rang shrilly in shock at the sudden contrast. The pressure lifted, but its toll remained in Alice's exhausted muscles, flooded with lactic acid. Shaking uncontrollably, Alice struggled to all fours and managed to reach the handle of the bathroom door. She proceeded down the hallway to her parent's bedroom. Foreboding filled her body, trepidation flooded her mind, terrible anticipation of what she might find pushed her onwards. She pushed the door and was met with no resistance. Standing beside her parents' bed was Niel, looking down proudly at the bloody, gory mess that had, only a few minutes ago, been Alice's beloved mother.

# CHAPTER TWENTY

## BRANDON

The following morning, as Stephanie awoke and looked longingly into my eyes, I could not find the strength to explain to her what I had experienced after our passionate lovemaking the night before. She nuzzled my neck, cuddled me as closely as she could, and whispered to me how much she loved me. Inexplicably, I could not feel the same way for her that I had over our several years together. I had not only no feeling of love for her, but no feelings at all—no fear, no anxiety. I was empty. Was my brain shutting down all my emotions in some kind of defence mechanism—completely overwhelmed by horror? Stephanie had fallen back to sleep on my chest, and looking at her peaceful breathing, her innocent beauty, I longed for my feelings to return to the early days of our relationship, of being so enthralled by each other than any worries were mere whispers, echoing on the horizon. Before meeting Stephanie, I never imagined that I would find someone who could care for me, despite all of my flaws. How could anyone ever love me, whilst I hated myself? But Stephanie did. I told her there was a darkness in me, that she should find what she sought elsewhere, with someone capable of returning the love that she so generously gave. She told me that there was plenty more light in me than darkness, and that she would always listen if I wanted to spill, yet I rarely had. I knew I had many problems – and whether or not they were due to my broken childhood, those were what I attributed them to, perhaps making excuses, perhaps not.

Over the years she had held me when I screamed in my sleep, my nightmares indiscernible from my memories. I used to have a strong hold on what was real and what was imagination, which is why I had never sought help for it. I had never known love like Stephanie had for me existed in the world, so, despite her recent unfaithfulness, I knew we would move forwards. I can get help. I can move on from my childhood and begin to feel emotions for her once again.

Much of my time as a child remained shrouded behind a wall of my own wilful ignorance, a wall that I needed to knock down if I was ever going to move forward, and to recover from what happened to me.

I gently lifted Stephanie's head from my chest and lay her down on the pillow. Being as careful as I could not to wake her, I threw on a dressing gown, picked up my phone and headed downstairs. I opened the browser on my phone and searched for the contact number of South East London care home and dialled the number. The receptionist on the phone sounded impossibly cheery for just after nine in the morning. She must have heard of the death of Patricia Harris, so I assumed that she either, like me, had no love for the woman, or was conducting herself incredibly professionally. Perhaps she hadn't worked there long enough to know her.

"Hello. Hackney East Care Home. How can I help you?"

"Hi. Umm, my name is Brandon Chapman. I used to live at your care home when I was younger, and I was wondering if you could give me the information you hold on me." I was sure they wouldn't still have my records and felt a little ridiculous requesting it.

"I see. Well, first of all, could you please provide me with your date of birth?"

"The fourth of April 1986."

"Thank you, Mr Chapman. Do you know what year you were with us until?"

"Umm... I moved out when I was sixteen, so I guess '02."

"OK, thank you. Now, all of our records from that long ago are with a central archiving company, so it will take a little while for us to get that for you. Also, there will be an admin fee of £50. Is that OK?"

"Umm, sure, yea." She took my credit card details for payment, and my address to send the files too, and told me that they would be with me within two weeks.

Hanging up the phone, I caught sight of the figure once again standing on the street opposite my house. I couldn't see his face, but could tell that he was smiling. I smiled back and offered a light wave, which he returned in kind. I could not describe my shift in feelings towards him. Somehow, despite what he had made me do, or made me think I had done, the figure had a hold over me, and I an interest in him. I began to feel something whilst staring at his mysterious form, not exactly fear which I might have had previously, but apprehension, and trepidation for what our future holds together. At that moment, Stephanie came down the stairs. The figure turned and walked away.

"Good morning, sexy," Stephanie purred, wrapping her arms around me. "I loved last night. It was so good to be so intimate with you again."

"I loved it too," I said without conviction, and kissed her full lips. "I called the care home I used to live in. They're going to send me the records that they hold for me within the next week or two."

"OK, that's great news. Any word of an appointment with the psychologist yet?"

"No. They did tell me there's a long waiting list. I heard on the news the other day that some people wait up to a year for mental health services. That's insane, no pun intended."

The next few days passed relatively easily, trips to the park with Lily, healthy meals at home with Stephanie, and no alcohol. My current lack of emotion served as a remedy for the constant fear I had felt previously, as good as passing out from drink. I saw the figure frequently, always nearby, watching, but never interacting. Stephanie appeared not to notice. Soon enough, her week off work was over, and, confident in the change in my drinking, she returned to work, leaving Lily and I at home on Monday morning.

I went to the kitchen to start preparing breakfast for Lily. She was happy watching Cbeebies as ever. She started speaking to someone, most likely one of the characters in Peppa Pig.

"Hello! Who are you?" My blood froze when I heard a reply.

"Why hello there Lily! I'm your daddy's friend. I dropped Lily's cereal bowl and ran into the sitting room.

"Why don't you go to sleep so that Daddy and I can talk?" The figure reached out and touched Lily's forehead with a fingertip, and she collapsed onto the carpet.

"What have you done?!" I shouted as I rushed him, intending to grab and shove him against the wall, before the familiar stabbing of hundreds of needles pierced my skin, without piercing it.

"Calm down, Brandon, she's sleeping, listen." I turned around and heard her lightly snoring. "We are friends, remember?" he said, smiling. "And it's not me you need to be worried about."

"What do you mean?"

"I showed you the future. Don't you remember? I didn't think you could forget that."

"Which future?"

"Stephanie, killing your precious little Lily. Haven't you realised? She's not the same woman you married, Brandon. First she has an affair, she lies to you about it, then expects you to just forgive by having sex with you. Next, she tells you that you have mental difficulties, and that you need to see a psychologist. Then she leaves you all alone, getting you back into your alcohol problem, almost killing you. And where is she now? You think she's at work? Pfft. Doubt it. She's probably already in bed with some other guy. She doesn't care about you. Or Lily. And she's going to get to you, the one place where you can still be hurt. She will kill her. You have to do something first."

"What do you mean, do something?"

"I mean, it's you and Lily, or her. That kind of something."

"How do I know I can believe you? Stephanie has never done anything to make me believe she could hurt Lily."

"She said she's at work. Call her office. She's not there, Brandon. She's with another man. She's fucking him and laughing at you. She's tormenting you. See you soon, Brandon," he said, and, knowing I couldn't stop him without suffering the needles, he turned and left the house.

His words nagged at me. Seeds of doubt sprouted, growing ever larger, blotting out any other thoughts, until I had no choice but to call Stephanie. Voicemail. I called her office. The receptionist said she hadn't seen her all day, but her schedule said she should be in. He was right. She was doing it again. If he was right about that, could it really be that what I saw in Lily's room was a vision of the future? Did Stephanie have it in her to murder her own child? Perhaps she truly was no longer Stephanie, but something wearing her skin, and my friend, through his own twisted means, was warning me? Impossible. Had to be impossible.

The rest of the day passed painfully slowly. A constant dialogue of doubt in the figure and opposing doubt in Stephanie played through my mind, and I had could not decide what to make of what the figure had told me. Not wanting to make any rash decisions that I could certainly come to regret, I stayed at home with Lily, watching the minutes pass by until eventually, at 8:15, shortly after putting Lily to bed, Stephanie arrived home. On stepping into the house, she must have sensed the aura of mistrust surrounding me.

"Where have you been?" I asked, the question loaded with suspicion.

"I've been at work. Why?"

"Have you? I tried calling you, you didn't answer your phone. I called your office, they said you hadn't been in. So, where have you been?"

"For Christ's sake, Brandon, I was at work. I had to attend an urgent last-minute appointment with a client in the City. I've been there with them all day. Have you been drinking again?"

"I haven't touched any. Not a drop. I don't need it anymore."

"Well, that I'm glad to hear. And I know it's hard for you to trust me now, after... what happened. But you can't start accusing me of having an affair every time I'm late home. If we don't trust each other, there's not much point in us even being together, is there?"

"You just don't seem yourself lately, and..."

"That's rich, Brandon, come on. You're the one who's constantly depressed, drinking, you've become a recluse. I want the man I married back." Her words hurt. In my almost emotionless state, the pointed tip of her words was dull and blunt, unable to pierce my defence.

"And I want my wife. I'm not even sure if I know who you are anymore. But I have to ask you something. How did we meet?" I felt ridiculous asking the question, and it may not have even worked, but if perhaps she was no longer my wife, and was something else in her skin, would whatever-it-is be able to answer the question?

"What are you talking about now? Why are you asking me that?"

"Please, just... tell me about how we first met." Anger flashed across her eyes.

"This is a ridiculous conversation," Stephanie said. "And I'm not going to be a part of it any longer."

If the figure had intended to make me doubt my wife and to cause further rifts between us, he was successful. It was as if a canyon was cracking open, rending the ground between us, whilst we stood on opposite sides, watching each other get further and further apart. Stephanie signed and appeared to have no energy to fight any further. She looked up into my eyes a final time before climbing the stairs, and for the briefest of moments, I could have sworn that I saw thick, black veins crawling out of her eyes and down her face.

# CHAPTER TWENTY-ONE

## ALICE

Light one second, darkness another. Repeating, flashing, light, dark. Streetlights? She must have been in a car. Burning pain seared her in the deepest parts of her mind. Who was driving? Barely able to keep her eyes open, she could not focus enough to discern any details of the driver, however, soon, he spoke.

"Didn't I tell you not to tell your mother about the baby?" Niel said. "You brought this on yourself. She could have lived." Alice was almost at a complete loss for words. She had hoped seeing the shredded corpse of her mother had just been another terrible vision, but Niel had confirmed the worst. Her mother was dead.

"How... how could you do that? What are you?

"You know what I am. And you wanted this, didn't you? Your precious Niel. I told you there would be conditions."

"I want the real Niel back." Alice's voice trembled and shook, sniffed between tears. "I want him back the way he was."

"Too late for that! Besides, were I to just leave now, what do you think would happen to Niel? He's dead. It's just me in here now."

Alice looked into the rear-view mirror and made eye contact with him. He was right, there was nothing left of Niel in those eyes.

"Where are you taking me?" Alice asked, frightened of the answer.

"Home. We're going to carry on as if nothing has happened. Because, you know now not to disobey me. You'll continue going to classes, but you won't talk to anyone about me, and you certainly won't tell anyone you're pregnant. And we are having this baby. If you attempt anything, you won't be allowed to carry on your normal life. I'll chain you somewhere and keep you alive just long enough for you to give birth. It really is in your best interests to do as I say. I hope you understand that." Alice didn't know what to say. Niel's voice had changed drastically, each word he uttered dripping with malice.

"What about the police? My dad will be back home tomorrow, and then they'll come looking for you."

"Alice, your dad isn't coming home tomorrow. I've already taken care of him as well. Again, your fault. I was happy to let him live. That big mouth of yours really does cause a lot of trouble. They won't find either of them anyway, unless they dig up their garden. And why would they do that? I booked them a one-way flight to Spain. Guess they felt like retiring early. So, you see, nobody is going to be looking for them."

Alice felt a deep, consuming sense of despondency. She felt like she was completely alone in the world. Worse – it was just her and Niel. He continued to drive towards Cambridge in silence, his breathing heavy and ragged. Darkness shrouded the car, the same pressure she had felt in the bathroom followed, less intense than before, but cloying, choking, crushing nevertheless. Alice allowed herself to succumb to despair. Her thoughts, grim, her options, compliance, or what? Suicide? She was sure she didn't have the strength left to even manage that. Compliance, then, for now, she decided. Perhaps he was wrong.

Maybe the police would find something. Would she be able to tell them herself? If he truly is going to take her back to her normal life, couldn't she just call them herself? Would he know what she was trying to do? She wasn't sure whether or not it would be worth the risk. There was nobody left that he could take from her, but the threat of being chained and kept prisoner by him was sure to cease any incompliant thoughts she would harbour.

Eventually they reached the city, and Niel drove through the familiar streets until he reached Alice's building.

"Now I'm sure I don't need to remind you, but you are going to continue as normal. We're still a couple, you're still a student, and you're not pregnant. If anyone asks anything about your parents, what do you say?"

"They're in Spain," Alice sobbed. Niel turned, grabbed the back of her head and brought her face within centimetres of his own. She could smell his breath, a disgusting, rotting smell. His touch was cold, lifeless. She tried to pull back away from him, but he was strong, and she was not. He kissed her, almost making her gag, kissed her long, hard, and to her disgust, slipped his tongue into her mouth, roughly assaulting her own with his. He reached out with his other hand and slipped it under her shirt. Alice let out a yelp as his cold skin made contact with her stomach, as cold as ice, and he moved further up her body, his fingers crawling their way across the familiar landscape of her chest. He grabbed her breast, squeezed it, caressed it, whilst continuing to kiss her. Finally, he let her pull away from him.

"Now fuck off. Go to bed, stay home all weekend, and go to class on Monday. I'll be watching and listening," Niel said, grinning.

Alice dreaded facing the stairs and the corridor leading to her flat. She knew the indescribable, explicit terror that she always felt, the visions she had experienced. Gingerly, she stepped closer and closer to the bottom of the stairwell. No fresh fear gripped her, instead, the opposite. Standing at the bottom, looking up to the top step, Alice instead felt a bizarre feeling of relief. She had no explanation for this shift in perception, from malignance to what could almost be described as joy. Each step she took towards her floor, however, shifted the balance back, her unfamiliar jovial feelings draining from her as the fear once more clotted in her veins. Running now, panting, rapidly tiring, she pulled her keys from her pocket; dropped them. She bent as quickly as she could and retrieved them. Daring a quick look behind her, she saw that the shadows from the stairwell were intruding into the corridor, pursuing her, the detestation she felt encompassing her as she unlocked the door and practically threw herself inside.

Back in her room, Alice sat on her bed, and found she had no strength left to even weep. She couldn't accept that both of her parents were gone. They had both, throughout her entire life, put her before themselves. She had taken this for granted until hearing stories from her classmates in secondary school. One had had both parents die while fairly young, most had parents who were separated, and, as such, had little time to spend with them, and yet another had a father who was in and out of jail for theft and fraud. She knew she had been privileged to have such parents, and a wonderful family life, and now it had been ripped away by whatever it was controlling Niel. She couldn't tell whether she was more filled by despair, or guilt, hate or rage.

She must have somehow fallen into a restless sleep, for the next thing she was aware of, the intercom was buzzing. All of her house-mates must have either been out, asleep, or too lazy to get up and answer the door. Alice was afraid to speak to anyone, but the bell buzzed and buzzed until she could take it no longer. Cautiously, she opened her bedroom door and peered out. No sign of anyone, including Niel. She slowly padded over to the intercom and answered it.

"He-hello?"

"Alice? Thank God. It's Charlie. Let me in."

"I... I can't. Sorry."

"Do you need to come in?" A second female voice asked Charlie over the intercom. The sound cut off. Alice stood frozen to the spot, terrified that Charlie was coming to her door, and whether or not Niel would know. The knock came, and Charlie's voice called through from the other side.

"Alice, please let me in. I haven't seen you for ages and I'm so worried about you. And we never spoke about Megan. Come on, let me in."

Alice didn't reply, standing frozen to the spot, hardly breathing.

"Look, I'm going to stay here until you let me. So just save us both some time and open the door now, please." Begrudgingly, Alice opened the door as narrowly as she could to allow Charlie to enter. She poked her head past the jamb and looked left and right. No sign of Niel still. But did he somehow know that Charlie was here, anyway?

Alice quickly closed the door again and turned to face Charlie. Alice was still wearing the same clothes from the day before, her skinny jeans now hung baggily from her legs, and her plain white t-shirt, normally flush against her stomach and stretched across her chest now hung from her shoulders like a flag at half-mast.

"Alice, are you okay?" Charlie asked, closely examining the physical changes in her friend since she last saw her. "Have you been eating? Is this because of Megan? I can't believe that she would kill herself. Why do you think she would have done that?" Alice heard footsteps in the hall outside, heavy, menacing, coming closer and closer.

"Shh! Be quiet for a minute," Alice ordered. Confused but compliant, Charlie stood silently, listening as the footsteps got closer and closer to the door, until they passed by and continued down the hallway.

"Alice, I'm worried about you. What are you so afraid of?"

"I can't tell you. You really shouldn't be here. He'll know."

"Who?"

"It really doesn't matter. Please, just leave and forget about me. We can't be friends anymore."

"I've already lost Megan. I'm not losing you as well. Honestly, I'm frightened that if I leave you here alone, you're going to end up going the same way as her. Go and lie down. I'll make you a cup of tea. You look like you need it, and we'll talk, okay?" Defeated, Alice staggered into her room.

Charlie searched the kitchen, amidst the mess left by Alice's housemates, for mugs that weren't full of cigarette ends or other detritus, but was unsuccessful. She needed to wash up two mugs before she could make any tea, and the sink was full of dirty plates and cups from who knows how long ago. She put the kettle on and managed to find a pack of PG Tips at the back of a cupboard. Once she had made the tea, she walked into Alice's room and found her, in the foetal position, on her bed, sobbing softly. She set the mugs down on Alice's bed-side table and sat on the bed beside her. The drawer was open, and Charlie saw the empty pregnancy test package nestled within. *That explains it*, she thought. *She's lost weight because she's stressed at getting pregnant and she's upset because obviously Niel hadn't taken the news of the pregnancy well and had probably ended things with her. Poor girl. Men can be so cruel.* She did, however, feel some relief at having become privy to the cause of Alice's behaviour. Not only was she pregnant, but of course, as Charlie was, she was still distraught at the loss of their friend.

"You don't have to talk to me if you can't right now, but I think you really should sooner or later. There's clearly a lot bothering you right now. For now, perhaps this will help." She got on the bed beside Alice, put her arms around her, and held her close. The pair lay together for several hours, individually dozing off and waking occasionally. No words were necessary, and they both gradually started to feel better – if only slightly. Charlie checked her watch. Shit. 5pm. She didn't want to leave Charlie, but she had a date with a classmate, Brad, whom she had been wanting to date for several months now.

"Will you be okay if I head off? If not, tell me, and I'll stay as long as you like," Charlie told Alice, feeling guilty at her own selfishness.

"Yes... I'll be fine." Alice replied. Charlie sat up, kissed Alice on the cheek, and got up to leave.

As Charlie left Alice's flat, she felt an irrational fear of the stairwell. She couldn't bring herself to descend them so, instead, she walked to the lift, pressed the down button, and waited in trepidation for it to arrive. A few seconds later, the doors opened, and she stepped inside, then pressed the button marked 'G'. The doors slowly closed, then the lift ascended rather than descended, and, frustrated, Charlie repeatedly pressed the 'G' button, the door open button, but none responded. Annoyed, she realised she would have to ride the lift to the top floor, then back down again.

Alice was worried that Niel would know Charlie had visited her. But she had obeyed his orders and hadn't told her anything about what he had done, that she was pregnant, and had somehow kept it from her that both of her parents were dead. She hoped he would not punish her further—after all, she had tried to get Charlie to leave.

Suddenly, an almighty crash shook the building from its foundations to the rooftop.

Charlie stood in the lift, on the top floor, waiting for the doors to close so that she could finally make her way down to the ground floor. She pressed the door close button three times, four, five, until they finally crossed her vision and met in the middle, encasing her inside. Suddenly, with a loud *twang* from above, the lift dropped. The cables had broken. Charlie was thrown into the air, and as gravity pulled the lift towards the inevitable, it smashed into the concrete below. Charlie was hurled back onto the bottom of the lift, which instantly crumpled, metal twisting, crushing her, cutting her. She was killed almost instantly.

# CHAPTER TWENTY-TWO

## BRANDON

After Stephanie headed up to bed, the ideas that the figure had planted in my head grew and grew, helped by Stephanie's – or whatever she was instead of my wife – inability or denial to recall or describe how we first met. I found myself walking into the kitchen, without conscious effort, and opened the familiar cupboard containing my beloved, hated alcohol. The warm, familiar oblivion called to me, but somehow I found the strength to resist. I needed to think straight. I had no idea who to trust; my wife, who has betrayed me at least once, or the figure, whose intentions I had no understanding of. I couldn't decide if the figure was lying, despite telling me truths previously, which meant that there actually *was* something inside of Stephanie, controlling her, corrupting her, to the point that the vision I saw of her came true. Or had Stephanie been the same as she always had been, minus the recent adultery, meaning that everything the figure said was merely meant to encourage me to succumb to his will? This didn't feel like a decision I could make. Either way, I was risking serious harm to Lily.

I didn't want to allow myself to think that Stephanie was capable, in any way, of truly being a risk to our daughter. She had never so much as raised her voice at Lily, even when she had been particularly trying. Before the birth, she was always concerned that once the baby came, she would suffer from postpartum depression. A colleague at work had told Stephanie that, after giving birth, she could feel no love for her own child when he was placed into her arms. She had said that instead she felt hollow, empty, blank, emotionless, and that the state had persisted for weeks afterwards. The thought terrified Stephanie. For weeks before she gave birth, she would speak about how she was worried she would be a terrible mother, that when looking at Lily for the first time, she too would look upon her as she did any other child, rather than the warming swell of the love that only a parent can feel for her child. Her worries were completely unwarranted, however. When Stephanie gave birth, she was in labour for over twenty-four hours. She was as exhausted as a person can be. Yet when the midwife placed Lily into Stephanie's arms, the expression on her face changed one-hundred-and-eighty degrees. Though she was exhausted, the instant love she felt for her first and only child eclipsed any other emotions.

And since the birth, she had continuously proved that she was a fantastic mother. Nothing had ever come first over Stephanie's career, not even me, until Lily. However, when Lily was one, and Stephanie had been back at work for a couple of months, she was offered a promotion by one of the partners of the law firm. It would entail working even longer hours than she currently did, and spending time at the company's other office in Manchester. Unable to imagine being away so much and missing even more of Lily's development that being a working mother entailed, she declined, at the surprise of her bosses and me.

Without allowing myself to think upon it any further, I crept up the stairs as quietly as I could. As I reached the landing and tiptoed along until I reached Lily's room. The door was open and, leaning against the frame, I could hear her soft, rhythmic breathing. With one hand I grabbed the bag full of baby essentials that we kept packed and ready to go, then gently padded over to her bed and picked her up as comfortingly as possible and rested her head against my shoulder. She stirred in her sleep but did not wake up.

Once back downstairs, I decided that I couldn't leave without writing a note for Stephanie. I found a scrap of paper and a red crayon, and whilst still holding Lily, scrawled the message:

*Stephanie, Lily and I are going away for a few days. I thought it would be nice for us both to get out of your hair. Don't worry, everything is fine, speak soon, Brandon x*

This hardly seemed enough to explain my abducting of our daughter and disappearing in the middle of the night, but what was I supposed to tell her? I knew that she wouldn't do anything crazy like call the police. I just needed more time to think about what to do without having Lily at risk.

I took my phone from my pocket and ordered a taxi as quietly as possible. Before placing the call, I hadn't decided exactly where I wanted to go. I panicked and asked to be dropped off at the Family Inn, a hotel that was part of a chain across London, known for cheap rooms and simple service. Before it arrived, I decided to walk to the cash machine around the corner and withdraw some money. In case Stephanie did go to the police, at least if they looked into my bank account transactions, they wouldn't see where I was staying if I paid cash. I was thinking like a criminal. It didn't feel good. However I knew it was necessary. I lay Lily down on the sofa, where she still slept, and quietly slipped out of the house.

Once I arrived back home, I rummaged in my pocket to retrieve my keys but struggled as one of my key rings had somehow managed to get itself stuck in my wallet. Once they were separated, I looked up and saw that the front door to my house was open. Sudden, gripping terror clawed at me. I knew that I had closed it. I rushed into the sitting room, and Lily was no longer on the sofa where I left her. Consumed by fear, I could no longer keep quiet, and screamed my daughter's name. I raced into the kitchen – no sign of her. The back door was still shut and locked. She hadn't left the house that way. I ran back through the front door and on to the street, still calling her name. Lights came on in many of my neighbours' windows, angry faces appearing in them. They were probably more concerned about the interruption to their sleep than the plight of their neighbour.

Lily knew never to leave the house by herself. She was a smart child, and shy. She wouldn't yet even climb the stairs by herself, let alone leave the house. Still, she must have done. Perhaps I woke her when I left the house, she wanted to follow me, went outside, and was grabbed by some opportunistic child snatcher. Unlikely. Or could the figure have seized the opportunity and taken Lily? Or had Stephanie been awake the whole time, and taken her before I could? I ran back into the house and, to my horror, found that the front door was now shut and locked. I still had my keys, and, fumbling, tried the key in the lock. It wouldn't turn. *I must be making a right spectacle of myself for the neighbours*, I thought, while banging on my own front door and ringing the bell incessantly. No answer. If Stephanie was inside, why wasn't she answering the door? And if she wasn't inside, does that mean that she has taken Lily? Finally, I realised that I was trying the back door key in the front door. They both fit both locks but will only turn in the correct one. Feeling foolish and worried that I was wasting time that Lily might not have, I found the correct key and went inside.

I ran upstairs, ignoring mine and Stephanie's room, sprinting straight to Lily's. The door was open, and there sat the empty bed. It wasn't another horrific vision.

I ran from the room and into my bedroom. Stephanie was in bed, sitting upright, eyes wide open.

"Stephanie!" I shouted at her. "Stephanie, have you seen Lily? She's missing. I... I'm so sorry. I only left her for a minute, and then when I came back, she had disappeared. I'm so sorry, baby, Stephanie?" She wasn't replying. Wasn't even hearing me. My heart skipped a beat. Was she that thing I saw that night again, instead of my wife? There was only one way I could think of to check. I gingerly reached out to touch her and, as I feared, as soon as my skin made contact with hers, my hand was pierced by hundreds of invisible needles, the pain causing me to instantly pull away from her. As before, there were no marks on my hand, but the pain lingered, repeatedly stabbing, pricking, and my hand clenched uncontrollably in response to the searing pain. I attempted in vain to touch Stephanie through the thick duvet, however the needles once again assaulted me, the duvet suffering no visible marks either. A heavy, booming pressure suddenly assaulted all of my senses at once. I could see thick black ripples, seemingly tearing at the very fabric of reality, twisting, turning, leaving great black fissures in their wake. I could smell a rancid, sulphuric, metallic odour in the air. My ear drums felt that they may rip apart any minute, *boom, boom, boom*, the echoing sound almost that of a giant evil heart, beating a substance much thicker than blood. My mouth was again overwhelmed by the taste of iron, as the pressure caused me to bite down hard on my tongue. And I could feel it, over every inch of my skin, every cell in my body, as real as if I were surrounded by every one of the Olympics fencing athletes, stabbing me relentlessly with their foils. Soon the power of whatever this was had me flush against the floor, whining in agony, blood and spittle dribbling from the corner of my mouth, completely and utterly helpless. The last thing I heard before completely succumbing to the evil presence was a voice, whispering, yet still audible above the crashing pressure. I could not tell who the voice belonged to. I'm not sure that I even heard it with my ears. Instead, it echoed through my mind.

"You're going to have to better than that, Brandon."

# CHAPTER Twenty-Three

## ALICE

The terrifying crash echoed throughout the entire building and sent Alice scrambling onto her bed as she retreated under the duvet. Despite not knowing exactly what had happened, she knew it involved Charlie. Both Alice and Charlie were being punished. Niel had somehow known and had kept his word on the consequences of betraying his orders. Suddenly, he was standing in front of Alice's bed.

"When will you learn, Alice? Why do you disobey me so? Haven't I killed enough people yet?" Alice found that she was unable to reply. Her mouth was dry, her throat tight, and her stomach wrapping itself in knots. She felt him sit down on the bed next to her, and she pressed herself against the wall, desperate to be as far away from Niel as possible.

"I guess I have to resort to more drastic measures to elicit your compliance. Tomorrow you're going to report to the dean at university, and you're going to tell him you're removing yourself from your course. I'll meet you there afterwards. Then you're going to come and live with me until you have the baby. Then, who knows? Maybe we'll have another!"

"Please... Niel, if there is anything left of you in there... please, don't do this to me. You loved me," Alice barely whispered from her hiding place. Niel laughed.

"I told you, he's dead. It's just me in here."

"And... who... what are you?" More laughter.

"I doubt if you can comprehend what I am. Come out from under there. Look at me. I'll tell you, and I want to see your reaction as I do." Alice gingerly pulled the duvet down to just below her chin. Niel smiled at her, and for a brief moment, Alice reminisced back to the time when the real Niel used to smile at her in that arresting way, his beauty and the warmth of his personality that even on their first meeting and completely won her over.

"I was born a few hundred years ago. I lived a short life. I was orphaned at a fairly young age. I forget how old exactly. Ten maybe. I didn't have anybody, so I got by the only way I could. I used to steal whatever I needed to survive, and I was good at it. Then I started to steal things that I didn't need. I used to pickpocket the wealthy bastards that treated me as if I were a piece of street furniture, I was less than nothing to them, not even worth glancing at, lest I spoil their appetite. Well, one day I got caught stealing from the wrong person—a policeman on his way home. Before he could cuff me, I pulled my knife that I always carried and slit his throat, from ear to ear. It felt so good. I'd never felt so alive. I got quite a taste for it, and pretty good at it, too. I killed twelve people before they caught me. I got overconfident, took fewer precautions before going hunting. Not long after that, they executed me. Hanging. Wasn't that bad really, pretty quick." Though his story would, under any other circumstances, lead Alice to believe that the story teller perhaps had several mental difficulties, or was speaking pure fantasy, Alice believed him. Niel was clearly not troubled by recounting to her however, the smile on his face ever present.

"Anyway, immediately after I died, I awoke. No language in the world can describe the place I woke into. The stories about hell being a dimension that is constantly aflame, ruled over by the devil, that's nonsense. There's no devil, only millions of human souls. The landscape, the structures, everything, is all the product of the imagination of the more powerful souls... and the human imagination can be *truly* horrifying. I happen to be one of those more powerful souls. I didn't enter Hell powerful though. I tortured many others, I created truly horrific torture rooms that they can never escape from. I became powerful enough to even leave hell. I'm the first soul to ever leave. It took a lot of strength to even communicate with you. It's taken all this time to get my strength back. Of course, I'm not as powerful here, but still considerably powerful enough to do as I please. And when our baby is born, when it's old enough to be corrupted, to commit hell-worthy sins, I'm going to drag it into hell with me. It will become as powerful as me, and we'll rule hell and earth together."

"Why me? Why Niel?"

"You asked for this, remember? I'm bound to him now. I'm not yet powerful enough to leave hell without being tied to someone up here. You asked for me, now you're stuck with me, for life. Though who knows how long that'll be?" Niel said, his grin increasingly more menacing.

"Do you understand now the situation you are in? Will you finally start obeying me? If not, well... I don't need you whole. Just alive long enough to deliver this baby, which you'd still be able to do without your arms, wouldn't you?" Alice was no longer able to reply. The pressure radiating from Niel suddenly pressed down on her, crushed every part of her body, internally and externally. Her thoughts vibrated through her mind, the pressure barely allowing her to even think. She screamed as she witnessed flesh-eating worms forming on her fingertips, chewing their way under her nails, through her fingers, consuming her arms, leaving her with nothing but bloodied stumps, the remains of her bones protruding. Niel stood, bent over the cowering, shaking Alice, and whispered into her ear.

"See you tomorrow morning, Alice." Niel, along with the pressure, had disappeared. She was alone and whole once more. She wrapped her arms around herself, overwhelmingly relieved that their loss had been only another horrific vision of what might come if she continued to disobey Niel.

Alice's thoughts became her own as Niel vanished. She thought about how her life had, in a brief time, been completely ruined. She had a loving family – now dead. She had a future, she would get a first in her degree, then a respectable job – gone. She had a boyfriend who she loved, who she was confident that she would've spent the rest of her life with – now dead, no, worse - dead and animated by the corrupt, nefarious soul. She was going to have a child – now she was terrified to give it life, to bring it into a world so wicked and evil. Niel's plan for her child could not come to fruition. She wouldn't let it. Though her child was not yet born, she had already come to love it.

Alice was overtaken by an inexplicable feeling of calm. Nothing worse than the recent events in her life could happen now. Any positive experience had been soured by an evil one – meeting Niel, who could've been the man of her dreams, ending in the release of some evil, twisted soul from hell, and her becoming pregnant was just the plan of that soul to become more powerful. Alice was now very aware of her own mortality. But that was all she had left to lose – her life. And what value did it now have? She had lost everyone she had loved, her parents and her friends. She had nothing left to live for, and the only act of love that she could give to her unborn child was obvious to her.

Sitting at her desk, Alice began to put her thoughts to paper. She wasn't sure if anyone would ever read it, or would care if they did, but it felt important to her to explain her behaviour.

*My name is Alice Hamilton. Whoever is reading this – you may not believe my words, but I swear, on my parent's souls, that it is true. My boyfriend, Niel Curtis, is no longer himself. He was killed in a traffic accident. A voice spoke to me promising to save him. I thought only of myself, not wanting to be alone without him, and I agreed. My act of selfishness destroyed Niel's soul, replacing it with a dark, twisted creature from hell. I heard this from his own wicked tongue. He killed my beloved mother and father. He killed my best friends, Megan and Charlie. He has threatened me with all manner of torture, and my life, once the child is born. I cannot, will not, give birth to this child, only to subject it to a life of horror and evil. You may think me cruel, insane even, but, this is an act of kindness. If there is anyone left in this world who cares for me: I am sorry. Please, forget me. Goodbye.*

Alice folded the note carefully, and hid it in her desk drawer, hoping that somebody besides Niel would find it. Ever selfless, she packed all of her belongings away, to save the effort of whomever had to clean up after her mess. Thinking clearly for the first time since Niel's accident, Alice had a small smile on her face. This was not the way she had imagined her life going, but it was considerably preferable to that which Niel was imagining for her. She now understood the meaning behind her visions, her fear of the dark stairwell. She did not understand why she had the visions – perhaps an unintended side effect by proxy of the soul possessing Niel's body, perhaps something else. She stood up straight, shoulders back, and walked towards the front door of her flat. As she went through the door and closed it behind her, she no longer felt any fear. Her mind was free, free to do what needed to be done.

She calmly left her flat, closing the door behind her. Her feeling of joy and relief built the closer she got to the staircase, that previously terrified her so. As she reached the top step, and looked down to the bottom, she was once again aware of the crushing pressure surrounding her, pulverising her senses. Niel was standing twenty feet behind her.

"Alice. I know what you're thinking of doing. Do you think you can get away from this, away from me, that easily?"

"You won't torment me anymore. And you won't have my baby," Alice told him, with strength and conviction behind her words, asserting herself for the first time, and possibly the last, in her life.

"If you do this, I will simply leave this body and enter you instead. Is that what you want? I would have immense pleasure tormenting you from within."

"I don't think you will. You're bound to Niel, aren't you?"

"Listen to me, you bitch, you're mine. For eternity. There's nothing you can do to escape me."

Alice took another step backwards, as Niel took a step forwards. Thoughts of her childhood flooded her mind. The warming, comforting love of both her parents swam through her veins, Alice almost in a state of euphoria. A time without worry, violence and evil. Her mother's arms wrapping around her. Feeling safe and protected while sitting on her father's lap. There was no greater joy than being loved as a child by parents as wonderful as hers, and Alice allowed herself to reminisce. Her final thoughts should be of home. Of love. Of a time in complete contrast to recent events. Thoughts that, if she believed in heaven, and deserved to ascend to its gates, would soon once more become her reality.

One more step backwards. The heels of her shoes were now over the edge of the top step. Niel was now running at her, his face an expression of thunder-made emotion. She felt victorious. That she was finally free and had robbed Niel of his evil intentions. Even as she allowed herself to drop, and sail through the air before colliding with the concrete below, she felt the love of her parents once more, surrounded by warm, glowing light, welcoming her into the world that lay beyond.

# Chapter Twenty-Four

## Brandon

I awoke dazed, unrested, and in my own bed, confused as to how I managed to get there. Stephanie was not on her side of the bed, and her phone wasn't sitting on the wireless charging dock as it usually was when she was home. I forced myself out of bed and checked the time on my watch. 7:15. She must have gone to work. As I stood, my brain felt like the very structure of it was collapsing in on itself, an excruciating implosion. I could see a strange, bright halo in front of my vision. I must've been suffering a migraine as a result of the assault I suffered last night. I realised that I couldn't hear Lily at play, which was strange for this time in the morning, normally she would be up and watching Peppa Pig, or creating her own Peppa Pig story with her soft toys. Stumbling down the corridor to her room took all my strength, what little I had. Her door was ajar, and, leaning against the jamb, I could see that she was in bed, fast asleep. My heart sank back into place, though was still beating in excess of a hundred beats a minute, as it had been continuously over the past couple of weeks. Surely, recent events had shortened my life drastically. I padded over to her small bed, kissed her on top of her head, then sat and leant against the wall. Immediately, I was asleep once more.

My dreams were haunted by Stephanie, or the thing that looked like Stephanie, but couldn't have been her. I saw countless ways of her torturing Lily, or myself, or both of us together. The most horrific, that will always be seared into my mind's eye, was Stephanie, veins snaking out from her eyes, crawling, creeping towards sleeping Lily, entwining her, piercing, Lily screaming, until she could scream no more, her own eyes now white, no iris, surrounded by black pulsating veins. As the veins penetrated her, she vomited a thick, black substance all over herself and her bed, until she stood, cackled, and I awoke, sweating, crying and shaking uncontrollably.

I scrambled to my feet and looked down at my sleeping daughter. I almost collapsed back down again when I saw that she was covered in the black vomit, just as she had been in my dream. My heart was threatening to tear straight out of my chest, beating so hard I was surprised to still be alive. I pulled my phone from my pocket and dialled 999 immediately.

"Hello, 999 emergency. Which service do you require?" The voice asked.

"Ambulance, now! My daughter, she has thrown up black vomit, and is unresponsive," I told her as calmly as possible.

"It's on its way. What is your name, please, sir?"

"Err... Brandon. Chapman."

"OK, Mr Chapman, what is your daughter's name?"

"It's Lily. Please, just get here as soon as possible. I couldn't bear it if I lost her."

"We'll be with you as soon as possible. Now, please, place your hand in front of Lily's mouth, and tell me if you can feel her breathing." I did as I was told, terrified of the result.

"It's faint, but I can feel her breathing."

"Good. Stay with her. Talk to her. And stay on the line. The ambulance will be with you any minute." Sure enough, I could soon hear the sirens in the distance.

"Lily, it's going to be OK, baby. Please, just... stay with me. I don't think I could cope if I lost you." She was unresponsive. I cleaned up her face and body and ran down the stairs to let the ambulance crew inside. It all happened so quickly. People usually say that time slows down in moments like these, but everything was a blur to me. Before I could even tell them what had happened, they had a breathing mask strapped to her face, and were transporting her into the ambulance. I climbed in behind them and sat with my head in my hands.

"What's wrong with her? Why did she throw up black sick?" I asked, already knowing the answer. There wasn't a medical explanation. It was all because of this damned figure... or Stephanie. As soon as she is better, I have to get away from all of this with her. If there is any getting away. Once we arrived at the Queen Elizabeth hospital, the doctors quickly took her away to the urgent care centre. I ran along behind, never letting her out of sight. Lily was still unconscious and was soon hooked up to all sorts of machines, only a few of which I knew the purpose of. Now the speed that time had been rushing forward, reversed, and whilst I waited to find out what would become of my only child, each tick of the large clock on the wall of the ward was separated by an insufferably long pause. This waiting was too much to bear. An hour passed. Two. Time crawled ever onwards, tormenting me. The doctors even appeared to be moving in slow motion. "Hurry up!" I wanted to scream at them but found myself unable to utter a sound.

"Brandon, I did tell you what you needed to do. If you'd had the balls for it, Lily wouldn't be lying in a hospital bed suffering. She could be tucked up safely at home, just like you. I'm feeling generous. Perhaps I'll allow you one more chance. Lily will get better on this occasion. Now, make sure you do it this time. I won't be helping you again," the voice of the figure warned me from inside my own mind.

"Mr Chapman? Mr Chapman!" one of the doctors was calling to me.

"Sorry. I was miles away... I can't bear to see Lily like this."

"I understand. However, I was about to tell you that Lily seems to be perfectly healthy. We were initially concerned that she may be suffering internal bleeding, however we've run several tests and found no cause for this, and she's not a haemophiliac. How is her diet? Do you feed her well?"

"Well, we try to as best we can. But she does love chocolate. We're always telling her off for sneaking it out of the cupboard."

"I see. Well ingesting a large amount of chocolate could certainly cause the vomiting and explain the colour of it as well. We're going to keep her in for twenty-four hours, make sure she gets plenty of fluids and she doesn't have any repeat episodes, then let you both go on your way tomorrow."

"I understand. Thank you, doctor. You're sure she's going to be OK? When will she wake up?"

"Daddy?" Lily whispered. The doctor smiled and closed the curtain behind him on his way out.

"Lily, baby. Are you OK?"

"I... I think so, Daddy."

"Do you know what happened? What made you ill? The doctor said you might have been eating too much chocolate. Were you sneaking some again?"

"No, I didn't. I promise. No choc-choc."

"So, do you remember anything else happening that might have made you sick?"

"There was someone in my room this morning." My heart stopped, and I felt the fissure tearing it apart. My little girl should not be being subjected to this. I have to put an end to it.

"Who was it, baby?" I asked as calmly as I could.

"Well, it was Mummy, but not Mummy. It looked like her, but she didn't talk like my Mummy, and she smelled funny too. So it couldn't really have been her."

"What did this person that looked like Mummy do?"

"She came over to my bed, and she was watching over me. Her hair was black and really long, and then it started moving all by itself! It was moving like worms, and it was crawling all over my face, and then down my throat, and that's all I remember." She was crying gently now, and I was amazed at how well she was taking this, and that she was able to articulate it all to me. Sometimes I forget she's only three. I know all parents say that their child developed quickly, but Lily seemed to possess a strength that I did not. Though terrified for her safety, I was also immensely proud of her character.

"Are you sure you didn't just have a bad dream?" I asked, not doubting, however, suggesting, hoping that she would accept it as a dream and move on from it.

"I'm sure. It was much more realer than a dream, Daddy. I could feel all the hair in my throat." I believed her. But that probably wasn't hair. I had a terrible image in my mind of those inexplicable black veins snaking their way inside Lily.

"Well, it's all OK now, baby. Daddy won't let anything bad happen to you." She was already fast asleep again, sleeping off the stress of the last few hours.

"Brandon!" Stephanie shouted from behind me. I hadn't told her what had happened, or that we were here. The hospital must have called her. "Why the hell didn't you call me?"

"I can explain. Lily... she, she thinks you made her ill." I told her about Lily's horrifying recollection.

"And you don't think she was just having a nightmare? You actually believe that I would hurt Lily... and, in such a strange manner?" Unable to contain myself any longer, I told Stephanie everything that the figure had told me.

"I know you've been going through some hard and... strange times lately," she said. "But I can't believe you'd doubt me. And I must say, I'm beginning to doubt your sanity if you believe that any of this is real. Maybe you should see someone while we're here. Get your head checked over." Stephanie's phone rang before I could reply, and she shot me a look before leaving the ward, speaking calmly once more. I could have sworn, when she turned to look at me, that there were once again black veins snaking their way from her eyes. I couldn't take this anymore. I had to do something. I felt my anger crawling through me, at an atomic level, seething, rising, encapsulating me in its reddening, murderous veil.

My actions were no longer under my own control. I was searching through the hospital supplies, knowing not what I was looking for but certain I would know it when I found it. I slipped out of the curtain separating Lily's room from the rest of the ward, and found it deserted, except for the nurse on reception, who was far too busy to notice me. There was a set of plastic drawers on wheels outside one of the other bays. When I opened the second drawer, I knew what I was looking for. I took it and tore it out of the plastic packaging. It felt good to succumb to the feelings of rage and violence. I didn't even attempt to question my actions, and obediently followed the dark path that was extending in front of me.

I crossed the threshold back into Lily's room. Still fast asleep. Sleeping like a beautiful angel. *Daddy is doing this just for you,* I thought. Stephanie's voice travelled through the air, raising the small hairs over my entire body. I dropped myself into the small, uncomfortable armchair beside Lily's bed, and pretended to be asleep, the prize I found hidden in my grasp, it's surgical steel cold against my sweaty palm. I could hear her ridiculous high heels *clack clack* as she came ever closer, echoing through the ward. No time to think about what I'm doing. Get it over and done with. It has to be done – for Lily. Yes, this was definitely the right thing to do. No turning back now. The final *clacks* sounded, and then the curtains opened. I kept my eyes tightly closed. I readied myself to leap at Stephanie and cut her throat with the scalpel.

# Chapter Twenty-Five

## Alice

Alice felt as though she were completely weightless. On all sides, if she even still possessed sides, shone a tunnel of brilliant light. There seemed to be no end, yet in the distance her own memories came toward her, flanking her as effervescent streetlights down a long road which leads to no destination.

She saw herself as a young child, one of her first memories. She was running from her father, giggling, as he chased her on his hands and knees across the living room. She tripped and hit her head on the floor and the shock made her cry until Kevin picked her up and kissed it all better, returning her to a fit of giggles.

This memory soon passed as she floated further down the endless tunnel. Next came along the memory of the Christmas when she got the Barbie Dream House that she had written on her letter to Father Christmas in big capital letters. A week before Christmas Eve, Julie had taken her out into the garden to burn the letter. That's how it gets to Father Christmas, she'd told Alice. The next morning, there was a huge parcel under the tree with her name on it. She could barely contain herself as she ripped off the paper to be met with the Barbie logo underneath.

She seemed to zip forward a few years and was now reminiscing about one of favourite memories from primary school. She loved to write and used to make up stories even when she was at home to give to her teacher, Mr Casson. He was a wonderful teacher and even marked Alice's extra-curricular writing at her request. *Another cracker from the pen of Miss Hamilton* he had written, and once Alice's parents told her what that meant, she was over the moon, and felt motivated to write story after story.

Several memories came to her quicker than the previous ones, her first sleep over at a friend's house, playing board games with her parents on holiday in Blackpool when it was raining. She saw her friend Jessica, who she had completely forgotten recently. She had stepped in to help Alice when she was being pushed around by one of the bigger girls in primary school.

Her first day of secondary school now, feeling terribly anxious on her first day, until one of the girls in the year above came up to her and told her she will look after her, as if she could see how scared Alice was. They never became close friends, but would always exchange a smile when they passed one another at school.

A few more years flew by, with more flashes of family holidays, barbeques in the garden. She passed her school exams with excellent grades, and her parents had opened her a bank account, depositing a couple hundred pounds to celebrate, with the promise that she saved it for when she was at university. Then Alice was opening the envelope that held the key to her future—her university acceptance letter. Her parents took her for an incredibly overpriced but wonderful dinner, with Alice radiating the success and happiness of the woman that she should have become in the future.

Suddenly there was music in this world that had been so bright, yet silent. She couldn't make it out at first as the beat echoed quietly from invisible walls, gradually becoming clearer until she recognised it as The Final Countdown, the song that had been playing when she had first met Niel. She was suddenly moving so much quicker down the tunnel, surrounded by the happy memories that she and Niel had formed together before he was struck by the sleeping driver who irreparably set their lives on a different course. She was reminded of that first kiss, so passionate that she felt herself falling for him right away. She felt the indescribable pleasure from their first time of making love, feeling like she could truly spend the rest of her life with this man.

The white light started to turn a dark red as more recent memories surfaced. Memories of the actions of the malevolent spirit that now wore his skin but bore no other resemblance to him. The music twisted and turned, mixed with what sounded like her own screaming, Niel's grating demonic laughter and then, for reasons she couldn't process, sirens. They grew louder and louder, as if approaching, encroaching on her private memories of her life. The red light instantly turned blue, then back to red, matching the sirens. Instead of floating towards the horizon that continuously moved away as she flew towards it, she felt herself being pulled backwards against her will. The memories she had seen going in reverse, all the way back to her father's kiss on her head.

A voice that she didn't recognise from any of her memories sounded from somewhere far away, muffled at first, but getting gradually clearer. Then a second, and a third.

"She's still breathing," said one panicked, unknown speaker.

"Don't touch her! Isn't that what they always say? We shouldn't move her. We might make it worse," an equally worried voice replied.

"Shouldn't we put her in the recovery position?"

"Step aside, please, let us get to her," a confident and authoritative voice commanded. "Does anybody know what happened here?"

"I got here just in time to see her land at the bottom of the stairs," the first voice said, cracking, as if holding back tears.

"Can you hear me, miss?" a voice asked. Alice didn't know they were asking her, but when no other voices responded, she said that she could. At least she tried, but she wasn't sure any noise came out.

"Don't strain yourself. You've had a fall, and we're going to take you to the hospital now. We'll do everything we can. Don't worry," the voice said, full of compassion.

The paramedics carefully loaded her onto a spinal board, strapped her in place and took her out into the cold, towards the ambulance. All of the lights and sound faded.

In Addenbrooke's Hospital, the accident and emergency team were preparing to receive Alice. They had been informed of the situation by the paramedics who attended the scene. The prognosis wasn't promising, as the incoming patient had suffered serious injuries in her fall down a long flight of concrete steps and was non-responsive. They weren't aware that Alice was pregnant.

The ambulance arrived at the hospital in almost record time due to a relatively small amount of traffic on the roads. Without wasting a moment, Alice was removed from the ambulance as soon as it arrived and was rushed to the waiting doctors. Dr Khan was the accident and emergency consultant on shift as Alice was brought in, who, luckily for Alice, was particularly specialised in spinal trauma. Dr Khan and the junior doctors began to remove Alice from the spinal board, at which point Alice woke up screaming.

The doctors rapidly re-strapped Alice to the board to prevent her from causing herself any more damage than she had already suffered.

There was a small open wound on her head, and her left forearm was visibly broken, bent almost ninety degrees.

"Niel! Is he here?" Alice screamed.

"Try not to move, sweetheart. It's important, until we know the extent of your injuries, that you stay as still as you can. Now, who's Niel? Is he your partner?" one of the nurses at Alice's side asked gently.

"Yes," Alice croaked.

"We'll try to call him for you and get him here," the nurse promised.

"No!" Alice's voice broke. "Please don't. I really don't want to see him. He's the reason I'm here."

"He did this to you?" the nurse sounded concerned, though she must hear similar stories depressingly often. Alice had slipped back out of consciousness, so wasn't aware that the nurse had asked one of her colleagues to call the police.

Alice's thoughts while she was separated from her body were dark and confused and were few and far between. When she was stood at the top of the stairs in the corridor, she hadn't expected to wake up again. She was pretty sure now that her plan had failed, and that she was still alive. If she hadn't managed to abort her own pregnancy with her leap down the stairs, she was terrified at the thought of what Niel would have in mind for her now. Would he be able to get to her in the hospital? He'd promised to torture her, to separate her from her limbs just for telling people that she was pregnant. Attempting to kill his child was sure to cause an apocalyptic wrath from the soul possessing Niel.

Suddenly, still unconscious, Alice became aware of Niel speaking to her through her mind.

"Oh Alice. What am I to do with you? You just don't learn. I am going to torment you from within for the rest of your life. It doesn't matter where you go, or what you do, you will never be rid of me. I'll make sure you never have another attempt at your life until you're no longer mentally capable of even considering betraying me again. I'll rend your mind, rather than your flesh. In my *considerable* experience, I find that to be much more effective. It's time to wake up now. Tell the doctors whatever you like. It doesn't matter. They're not going to believe you. Talk soon!" Niel said, almost cackling.

Alice opened her eyes. The first thing she was aware of was that she couldn't move. A strap kept her head in place, and her hips and legs were held fast.

"N...nurse?" Alice managed. Seconds later, a female face with a warm expression stared back down at her.

"Hello Alice," she smiled. "Please try to stay still for me. This isn't going to be easy to hear, but you've suffered some serious damage from your fall." Alice wept. Not only had she been unsuccessful in taking her own life, but she had survived and possibly suffered permanent injuries. She was suddenly aware that something was terribly wrong with her body.

"I... I can't feel my legs! Why can't I feel or move my legs? Have you given me something?"

"I'm afraid you've suffered serious damage to your spine, Miss Hamilton. It's too soon to tell at the moment, but from what we've seen of your injuries so far, I'm very sorry, but I need to make you aware that there's a possibility you won't be able to walk again." Alice couldn't hear anything else the doctor had said. She wasn't sure how long the doctor was talking to her until she suddenly realised she did not yet know the fate of her unborn child.

"What about my baby? Did it survive?"

"We... we didn't know that you're pregnant, Miss Hamilton," the nurse said, clearly very concerned. "We haven't noticed any bleeding, which may be a positive sign, but we're going to need to run tests immediately." The nurse practically ran from the room.

Within minutes, Alice was surrounded again by a team of medical staff. A male nurse carefully lifted Alice's gown above her concave stomach and applied ultrasound gel to her skin. The ultrasound technicians were preparing the machine, and Alice held her breath as she waited to be informed of both her child's and her own fate.

# CHAPTER TWENTY-SIX

As Stephanie passed the curtain and I saw the look of despair in her eyes, I slipped the scalpel into my pocket. I couldn't do it.

"I'm sorry," I said, lacking the strength to look her in the eyes. "But everything I've told you is true, I'm not delusional. I am being stalked by this figure, and he's making me see these terrible visions of the future, making me think I've killed people. I don't know why, but I'm going to prove it to you. I can't stand having you think I'm losing my mind."

"And how are you going to do that?" Stephanie asked. An idea came to me.

"I often see him outside of our house, as if he's waiting for me to snap. I'm going to buy some CCTV cameras. I'll get him on video, then you'll believe me, I hope."

"I don't know if that's necessary Bran..."

"It is necessary. Even if just to prove my sanity to myself."

Stephanie and I spent the next twenty-four hours in shifts at Lily's bedside, spending little time together and offering few words to one another. After Stephanie had been home to rest for a few hours and then returned back to the hospital, I made my way home, but stopped by at a hardware shop first. I wandered over to the home security department and found a set of cameras that connected over Wi-Fi, and that I could watch from my phone. Perfect. Not being a man particularly skilled in DIY and having no tools, I picked up an electric drill, some screws and screw bits, hoping that's all I'd need to fix the cameras in place. I was about to head to the till when I noticed some baby monitors on a shelf. We hadn't used a monitor for over a year with Lily, but having seen it, I now couldn't shake the idea that I needed it to make sure nothing happened to her.

I headed to the till and made my purchase.

"Congratulations," the smiling, chubby man behind the counter offered.

"Sorry?" I asked, confused.

"New baby?"

"Oh, yea, that's right. Can't be too careful."

"Right you are. OK, so, that'll be a hundred and fifty-one pounds, please." I handed over my credit card, hoping I wasn't at my limit. The printing receipt confirmed that I wasn't yet completely broke. I thanked the friendly assistant and headed home as quickly as I could to install the cameras.

Once home, I took a chair from the dining room to stand on, as my height left me a little short of reaching the top of the porch overhanging the front door. I plugged in the long power cord of the drill into the nearest socket in the hallway and took my first shot at using a power tool. I hadn't got a strong enough grip on the first try, sending the drill skidding across the brickwork. I had another go and managed to drill three holes in the correct places. I surprised myself as I fitted the screw plugs and screwed the camera into place. Setting it up and connecting to Wi-Fi was easy enough, and soon I had a view of the driveway and road in front of the house on my phone screen.

Next I set up the Wi-Fi baby monitor, which also had a camera. I placed it on the dressing table, and soon enough, I could also see Lily's bed on my phone. I wished I had done this sooner. Perhaps Stephanie wouldn't think of me as a total wreck of a man. I went back downstairs, and almost against my own will, walked into the kitchen, and grabbed the full bottle of gin from the kitchen cupboard. Staggering into the sitting room, I collapsed into the sofa, and before I could even unscrew the cap, I'd fallen asleep.

Thankfully, I awoke a couple of hours later after a dreamless sleep, with no sign of the figure. It was time to head back to the hospital and let Stephanie come home for the night. The short drive was uneventful, and I parked and paid the ridiculous hospital car park fee. I found Stephanie in the uncomfortable armchair beside Lily's bed, both fast asleep. I took a moment to study her. She looked like she had aged over the last few weeks, dark circles evident under her eyes, stress lines on her forehead and her skin lacked the radiance she usually had.

"Bran, you scared me," Stephanie gasped as she awoke.

"How's Lily doing?"

"She seems her normal self, really. We watched some TV, I read to her, and she had some tea, then fell fast asleep. There doesn't seem to be anything wrong with her, so we'll take her home in the morning."

"OK, well, get yourself home. You look like you could use some proper sleep."

"Oh, well, thanks for that," Stephanie said sarcastically.

"You know what I mean," I countered.

"Can I trust you here with Lily? How are you feeling?" Stephanie asked with genuine concern.

"Of course you can. I'm fine. I've already installed the cameras at home. I hope we don't see that figure again, but if we do, hopefully you'll believe me. And if we do, we need to get Lily away from the house. Maybe we can stay with your mum, as fun as that would be. Or even sell the house and move somewhere else."

"Can you hear yourself? You want to sell the house because you think someone is feeding you visions of how Lily is going to die? I can't talk about this anymore right now. I am going to go home, and to be honest, I'm only trusting you with Lily because she's in the safest place."

Stephanie left the ward, but her words kept burning me. I sat in the solid chair, and with nothing else to do, pulled my phone from my pocket and opened the news app. There were several articles about Patricia Harris. Someone had already been arrested for the murder, a man of about my age who apparently had been abused by her whilst under her care in the same orphanage as where I grew up. I always hated that woman. Perhaps she got what she deserved, I thought. I was beginning to believe that I wasn't responsible for the murders. I had no idea of the motives of the figure, for encouraging violent thoughts in me and making me believe that I had committed them, though.

A ping from my phone distracted me from my thoughts, and I realised I had received an alert from my security camera app. Movement had been detected. I quickly touched on the notification, and within seconds a live stream of the front of my house greeted me. It was just Stephanie pulling into the driveway. She sat in the car for a few moments, her face hidden from me in the darkness. But she wasn't alone. Standing on the other side of the street was the figure. Terrified, I called her immediately.

"What is it, Brandon? I just got home."

"Don't get out of the car," I warned. "Look in the mirror. He's right behind you, on the other side of the street."

"Yea, I can see there's someone there, but it's just some guy. He's not doing anything."

"Please believe me. It's him. Drive away. You don't know what he's capable of."

"I'm too tired for this. I'm going to bed. You should try to sleep as well. You clearly need it," Stephanie said before hanging up.

I switched back to the security app and saw Stephanie getting out of her car. The figure crossed the road and approached her. Fear enshrouded me, contorting my body, tensing every muscle in my body as I watched remotely, helplessly. As he got closer and closer, static began to take over from the previously clear image provided by the camera, until I could see nothing else.

I couldn't see that I had any other choice. I threw Lily's bag over my shoulder, took her into my arms and went to leave the ward.

"Excuse me, sir," said one of the ward nurses. "Where are you taking her?"

"Home. I have to get home. It's an emergency," I told her without stopping.

"I think it would be best if you kept her here, sir, as she is to be kept on hydration."

"I'll make sure she gets enough water."

"You are free to take her if you think that's the best decision, but I would advise against it," she said, rather sternly.

"She's my daughter. I'll decide what's best for her." I was losing my patience.

"Like I said, it's your decision. I need you to sign a form before you take her, though, to remove any responsibility from us." She led me to the front desk, and I filled the form out as quickly as possible, signing my usual illegible squiggle.

I strapped Lily into her child seat and floored it out of the car park. Throughout the entire journey, I tried to call Stephanie every thirty seconds, with no response. Panic rose in my throat until I could taste the bile. What would I do if he's hurt, or worse, killed Stephanie as he threatened? He wanted me to kill her, tried to convince me that it was her who was evil, possessed, murderous in intent. There was no denying his manipulative prowess, but I was falling for it no longer.

The darkness surrounding the car began to physically manifest itself into veins, darker than the night itself, visible only in the lack of any light whatsoever. They pulsed, snaked their way out of the night, seething, writhing towards the car, maintaining a similar speed. I pressed the pedal to the floor of the car but the veins, sprouting malevolent thorns, oozing the terrible substance as they went. They made no attempt on my car, but followed me, watching without eyes. Other drivers passed me without incidence, both unaware of the veins and able to pass through them as though they were formed of pure terror and maliciousness rather than a physical substance.

Finally, I arrived at home and found no evidence of anything terrible happening yet. I removed Lily from the seat as gently as I could, left the car unlocked, and entered my home. Stephanie was sat on the carpet of the living room, her head resting on her knees. I lay Lily gently on the sofa, and though I was afraid of being subjected once more to the invisible needles on touching her, I tentatively grabbed her by the shoulder. Nothing happened.

"I'm sorry, Brandon. You were right. He's... I don't know what he is, but he's not human."

"What happened?" I begged, my fear slightly negated as my wife was alive and responsive.

"He told me that if I don't kill Lily within the next seven days, he will. And I believe him. He... oh god... his eyes were pure white. He had no irises, but he could see me. Then these... veins, I guess they were, came out from under his eyes until they pierced my own. I couldn't get away from him, I couldn't move, and I saw him killing her. It was horrendous. I can't even tell you what he did to her. I won't. It's too terrible. What are we going to do?"

# Chapter Twenty-Seven

## Alice

Alice didn't have to wait long.

"Great news," the ultrasound technician said with a smile. "There's a pulse. Your baby is alive." Alice decided that, though there was nothing she could do whilst in hospital to end her own life and rob Niel of the pleasure, she could still do something about the pregnancy. Even as she was having thoughts of abortion, she heard his voice inside her mind.

"I know what you're thinking. If you even bring up an abortion, I'll kill anyone you discuss it with. They won't even have the chance to record that you said that. Then, I'll kill their family. Do you want that on your conscience?" Alice swallowed her words before they came out of her mouth.

"Now, Mrs Hamilton," said Dr Khan, "the police have been waiting to speak to you. They would like to speak to you about what happened, as you told the nurse that he's the reason you're here." It was DCI Waters that Alice had spoken with after Megan's death. She was alone.

"Hello again, Miss Hamilton," Waters said, concern etched into her face. "I'm glad to see you're awake, and I'm terribly sorry to hear the news of your injuries. Could you please tell me what happened?"

"I don't remember," Alice lied, her voice devoid of emotion, sounding as flat and empty as she felt.

"I hear that you told the paramedics that your fall was due to your partner, Niel. Is that true?"

"I told you, I don't remember."

"Alice, I understand if you're afraid to tell us the truth. In fact, that's how most people respond to cases of domestic violence. But if your partner did this to you, you need to tell us. You don't want him hurting anyone else, do you?"

Alice knew she couldn't tell the police woman anything without risking another murder being committed by Niel. Again, as she was thinking this, Niel spoke to her once more.

"Tell her, go on. I won't kill her. Tell her. She won't drop this. And it makes no difference to me. It'll definitely hurt you a lot more than it will me. Tell her."

Needing the release of confiding in someone else, but simultaneously unsure of how to articulate everything that had happened, Alice decided to start from the beginning. She spoke of everything, from how she had first heard the voice offering to save Niel, to how his behaviour had changed, the visions she had seen, his threats. She told him what Niel really is now instead of being himself, and how she had felt that taking not only her own life, but that of her unborn child was the only option she had left to her. Waters' expression changed from concern, to pity, to confusion as she realised that Alice truly believed her impossible story. Finally, after Alice had poured out her heart, the detective broke her silence she had maintained whilst listening.

"I see, Miss Hamilton. Thank you for confiding in me. Do you still wish to take your life, or that of your child?"

"Yes. If I don't kill myself, Niel will do it, and it will be so much worse. And I am even more terrified of what he will do to the baby."

"I see," Waters repeated, unsure of what else to say. "I need to go and speak to your doctor for a moment, Alice. I'll be right back, okay?" Alice offered no response.

Waters strode over to the front desk of the ward. Her usual confident gait slowed as she contemplated Alice's words. She knew she was going to have to speak to someone at the hospital better equipped to deal with Alice's suicidal and infanticidal admission, and she was fairly sure where it would lead.

"Can I speak with the on-call consultant psychiatrist regarding Miss Hamilton, please?" Waters asked the incredibly busy looking nurse. She sent a page to the consultant, Dr Qin. Waters took a seat and waited. Fifteen minutes later, the telephone rang, and the receptionist answered.

"Hello, can I help?" the nurse at reception asked. "Ah, Dr Qin. Thank you for getting back to me. There's a police officer that would like to speak to you regarding a patient. Okay, that would be great, thank you." The receptionist crossed the waiting area and informed Waters that Dr Qin would be with her in half an hour, once she had seen her last patient in her outpatient clinic. Waters passed the time with thoughts of Alice and how much she had changed since their last meeting.

Meanwhile, Alice felt nothing. She was drained, exhausted, an all-encompassing lethargy, except for when Niel spoke to her once more.

"I can't believe you actually told her. How stupid are you? Now they're going to lock you up in a mental institute. You think you can make those kinds of claims and then go back home? This is perfect," Niel practically sang, his words dripping with nefarious contempt. "Now you're going to be right where I want you. I told you I would destroy you mentally. Where better for you to be?"

Alice now felt a complete despondency. She was separate from her body. This was the only defence that she now had from anything that Niel could do to her. She could see herself lying in the hospital bed, broken, both physically and mentally, and could not recognise it as her, she had changed drastically in such a short time. She saw the curtains surrounding her bed being pulled open, Waters and an Asian doctor approaching her, talking to her, but heard no sound.

"Miss Hamilton, this is Dr Qin. She'd like to speak to you."

"Hello, Miss Hamilton. The detective here has informed me of what you told her. Is she correct that you did this to yourself, because of what you think your partner will do to you? Alice didn't respond. She was still out of body, no longer caring what happened to her.

"Miss Hamilton?" Waters and Qin exchanged concerned glances. "Alice, can I call you Alice? Detective Waters has told me that you still have the intention of taking your life and your child's. Is that correct?" Alice could hear Niel's cackling as the pair spoke to her silently.

"Alice, if you won't talk to me and deny that this is the way you feel, I'm afraid that I have no choice but to request that you be sectioned to avoid harm to both yourself and your unborn child." Still, Alice heard nothing, said nothing.

The doctor and the detective eventually gave up on trying to question Alice. She had made no attempt thus far to refute the claims, or even to make eye contact or any other indication that she was mentally present.

"Please, just go. Leave me alone." The two professionals assumed Alice was talking to them.

"If that is what you wish, Alice, we will leave you alone for now."

"Why are you even doing this to me? I was a normal person. Now look at me." The detective and the doctor both shared similar facial expressions at their confusion and concern. Qin was taking notes of everything that Alice said. Of course, they could only hear Alice's side of the conversation.

"Yes. OK. I want this baby. There. Now please, don't kill them." Alice fell silent once more. Doctor Qin left the room once she was confident Alice would not respond any further, and, with a heavy heart, made a telephone call.

The spirit inside Niel felt good. Powerful. He enjoyed being in this body. Girls looked at him, wanted him. Men stepped out of his way, intimidated by him. Yes, he'd picked a good body. He hadn't planned to become a father, and of course, technically it wasn't his, his or her real father is the dead body that he is riding, but, they would be part of the same bloodline as the body he had taken over. That meant a few things.

Though loathe to admit it, in some ways, he missed being human. And being a human in this time, compared to his own, was so much better. Instant gratification was available, no matter what you hungered for. Sex? He was certain that most of these girls would happily take him home with little to no effort on his part. Violence? It's Saturday night in a student city, the majority of people were much closer to inebriation than sobriety, looking for an excuse for a fight. Then there was the food, endless takeaways, restaurants, burger vans, food that he had never been privileged enough to try in his own lifetime, but now, with Niel's healthy bank account and an even healthier appetite he could gorge until he was completely satiated, in every respect. Yet being in a human body had its limitations. He no longer had the strength he possessed in hell, the power of an evil imagination conjuring the implements and prisons of torture. But he wasn't powerless. His imagination was still strong, and though no physical manifestations would be possible, he knew the flaws of the human mind. How open to suggestion it was, how easily manipulated, and he could cause such terrible visions within them. His body was already dead, so couldn't be killed again.

He hungered for sex and violence. On his way to the student union bar to get his fill on the former, a drunk student accidentally walked into him.

"Watch where you're going, mate," the student yelled.

"Mate? I'm not your fucking mate," Niel replied, his priorities now switched. The street was fairly busy with the freshman students heading to the bars early, but Niel was unconcerned about having an audience. He ran at the unfortunate young man, tackling him to the ground. He grabbed the hair on the back of his head, and with all his strength, slammed his face into the tarmac once, twice, three times. He stood and stamped on the back of his head repeatedly, though he was already dead. None of the horrified onlookers dared to help and ran into the nearby bars or take away restaurants for help. Above Niel, and one door down, was a CCTV camera, designed to cover the entrance to the bank, and had captured the murder. Police officers had already been informed.

He decided that, as much as he wanted to go and find a girl, he probably wouldn't have much luck with his hands, shirt sleeves and shoes covered in blood. Instead, he headed back home, fully intending to clean up and head back home. Shortly after he arrived and washed the thick blood from his hands and changed his clothes, there was a buzz at the intercom. His roommates weren't home. It rang several times, and out of sheer curiosity, he decided to answer.

"Hello?" He spoke happily, still high on the temporary fulfilment of his violent needs.

"Police. Open the door now or we'll break it down." Shit. Police? Not them again. The reason why he ended up in hell in the first place. He had no intentions of going with them, but also knew that there would be too many of them for him to deal with. His flat was on the first floor, a relatively low drop to the ground, and it was at the back of the building. With only a single punch, he smashed the window, then leapt out and ran.

Alice saw two new people she hadn't seen before entering the private room that she had been transferred to, along with Doctor Qin, whilst her out-of-body experience was still ongoing.

"Hello again, Alice," Qin said softly. "This is my colleague, Doctor Black," she said, indicating to the rather stern, official looking doctor. "And this is Rosalia. She's a social worker." Qin gestured towards the woman with a headful of red hair. "Please try to listen to me, Alice. This is important. We three have decided, based on what you've told us and the behaviour that you're exhibiting, that it's in your own and the public's interest to detain and section you under the mental health act. We're going to be keeping you in the hospital for now, under a locked ward. We have the authority to hold you for up to six months while we offer you treatment, at which point hopefully we will review your case, and we hope to see an improvement in you by then."

Alice had heard everything this time but was powerless to even attempt to respond.

"Do you have any questions for me at this time, Alice?" No response. "In that case, we'll take you up to your new ward now." Alice watched as her broken body was lifted and placed gently into her wheelchair and taken away.

# Chapter Twenty-Eight

## Brandon

Stephanie and I didn't get any sleep that night. We both lay awake, with Lily in between us, each of us with a knife in hand, though unconvinced of what protection it may offer. The night was long, and though there was no sign of the figure, the pressure the figure exudes pressed upon both of us.

"I love you," Stephanie said, still shaking with fear.

"I love you too," I replied, realising how long it had been since we'd exchanged those words. I suddenly felt overwhelmed by my feelings towards her. She and Lily were the only good things that had happened in my life. Before I met her, I was merely existing, my life was going nowhere, and I could count my happy memories on one hand. I never thought that I could be happy, yet Stephanie had proven otherwise. The fact that I could still, in this terrible situation, still feel the slightest sunrise of hope on the horizon was a testament to her. To the love that she had shown me through our marriage, and, despite the affair that she'd had, I knew that if we made it through this, all three of us, we could somehow return to some sense of normality.

"In the morning, you're going to take Lily and drive. Drive far away, stay in a hotel and don't call to tell me where. We can never know if he's listening or not. Each morning you're away, move to another hotel in another town. I'll deal with this somehow."

"What are you going to do? How can you do anything?"

"I'm not sure. I'll get the police involved somehow. Perhaps if they're watching the house, they might be able to catch him before he does anything again."

"I don't know, Bran. What can the police possibly do against someone – something like him?"

"It's the only choice we have. I'm not going to argue about it, you have to leave tomorrow."

"But how can I leave you here with him? What if... what if I never see you again?"

"That won't happen. He doesn't want to kill me, I'm sure. He could've done it a thousand times by now if he did." Stephanie knew my mind was set and argued no further.

At seven o'clock, Lily woke up.

"Mummy? Daddy? Why aren't I in bed?

"Well, I had to get you ready. We're going on a holiday," Stephanie lied through a smile.

"Oooh. Where are we going?"

"It's a surprise," Stephanie said, while choking back tears. "Daddy is going to stay here for a few days, but he'll join us soon, won't you, Daddy?"

"Of course. I wouldn't miss it," I said, whilst not being as successful as Stephanie in damming my tears.

Once Stephanie had prepared a suitcase with clothes for herself and Lily, we headed down the stairs. We kissed for as long as we could with Lily present, both of us weeping. Then, Stephanie put Lily into her car seat, got in herself and started the engine. She didn't break eye contact as she sat, trying to find the strength to leave. She blew me a kiss, mouthed 'I love you', then drove away. I prayed that this wouldn't be the last time I saw her, though had little doubt that it would be.

Not knowing what else to do, I planned my call to the police. What would get them to watch the house without me telling them the truth that they would unquestionably not believe? Drugs. I picked up my phone and dialled 101, the non-emergency police number.

"Hello, police. Can I help you?"

"Hi. I'd like to report a property that the owner appears to be dealing drugs from." I gave my own address.

"And what makes you believe this crime is taking place?"

"I live nearby. There's always people coming and going at all hours. They are only inside for a minute or two, and the house always stinks of cannabis."

"I see. Thank you for reporting this to us, sir. We'll follow this up."

"What are you going to do?"

"We'll keep an eye on it, sir. Is there anything else that I can help you with?" she asked, and I told her there wasn't, unconvinced that anything would happen as a result. I decided that I would call again later and pretend to be someone else reporting the same crime.

I sat in my chair, with no other plans on what to do, the knife beside me. My phone pinged. I hoped that it wasn't Stephanie telling me where they were going. It wasn't, instead there was a notification from my security app, which meant there was movement outside the house. Not being brave enough to go and look for myself, I opened the app. I breathed a sigh of relief. It was the postman, delivering a thick envelope for me.

As it dropped onto the carpet, I realised it must be the information I requested from the orphanage. I didn't hesitant to tear it open and

find out what information they had on me, though I wasn't as convinced as Stephanie was that there would be anything of much interest
inside. Turns out I was wrong.

Within a couple of weeks of my arrival at the orphanage, a young
couple in their late twenties adopted me. They had found out that
both of them were unable to have children of their own. I had spent six
months with them, up until I was nine months old. Wanting to truly
make me a part of their family, they applied to have my name changed,
and that's when my name changed from Brandon Hamilton, my birth
name, to Brandon Chapman.

I read in horror about my mother. Her name was Alice Hamilton
and, according to the most recent notes in the file, she had been
confined to a secure hospital ward for her own safety since before my
birth. My heart skipped several beats when I read why she was being
kept there.

*'Attempted to take own life and that of her unborn child by throwing
herself down a flight of concrete steps. Described her reasoning for this
as wanting to escape her partner, who was in fact no longer her partner.
Exhibited delusions that she "made a deal" with a voice that spoke to
her inside her head, offering to save her partner's life, with the caveat
that he will not be the same person she once knew. She stated that because
she accepted, he is now tied to her partner. She also stated that what she
calls 'the spirit' that was then possessing her partner's body informed her
that his body was dead and was only being kept alive by his presence.
Indicated that he informed her he is a soul that escaped from hell and
described several delusional visual and auditory hallucinations which
she described as 'demonic'. She described episodes such as seeing impossibly large black veins, menacing in nature, in a variety of settings,
believing them to be caused by her former partner with the intent of
threatening her co-operation. She also described seeing said partner with*

*eyes of pure white, lacking any irises, with black veins manifesting from his eyes.*

*'After the first six-monthly review, Alice's behaviour and disposition have not improved. She has exhibited no further wish to take her child's life, however she has indicated that her former partner, Niel Curtis, still communicates with her, that she hears his voice inside of her head at all times of the day. She has made no attempt at harming any of the staff or other patients on the ward, however does not take her medication and will not eat unless forced to do so. After this first review, the decision has been made that it is in the patient's own interests to keep her in the secure ward of Addenbrooke's hospital.'*

I couldn't read anymore. This was too much to take, even after suffering everything that had happened recently. That's why the figure showed such an interest in me. I'm his son. Well, more accurately, the son of the person the figure used to be, before being controlled and corrupted by an evil spirit. What he wanted with me was still a mystery, however. What must he have done to my mother for her to decide that her only option was to try to kill herself while pregnant with me? The fear that I had felt almost non-stop recently was replaced with rage. My poor mother. She had been subject to even worse terror than I had from what I could tell, to a suicidal state, only to then be locked in a hospital and treated as if she were a criminal, as if she were insane. I had to make this bastard pay for what he had done to my family, especially now that I knew to what extent. But how? If he is what my mother said, I don't think the knife by my side will do much good. I was hopelessly unprepared, and undoubtedly running out of time before he surely made good his threats of killing my wife if I refused to do it myself.

I dared to take a look at the security app on my phone for signs of the figure. I refused to think of him as my father. He was long dead. The street looked clear, so I went to the window and opened the curtain for a better look. It was a bright and clear day, and everything looked normal. No sign of him anywhere. There was, however, a car parked a few doors down on the other side of the street. I could see two people sitting in the front seats, but as I watched, they didn't drive off or get out of the car. Perhaps the police had, in fact, sent a car over to watch the house for signs of a possible drug deal? I hoped so.

My thoughts shifted to Stephanie and Lily. Was sending them away a good idea? Surely if I had no idea where they were, he wouldn't know either, though this is someone whose power I have no comprehension of. Would it have been better for us all to stay together? I considered calling Stephanie and asking her to come back home, or to tell me where she was going so that I could go and be reunited with my beloved family. It wasn't worth the risk. Our only chance of keeping them safe was to keep them hidden.

I needed a drink. I went without thinking of what I was doing to the cupboard in the kitchen, grabbed the full unopened bottle of gin and a bottle of tonic. I threw a couple of ice cubes from the freezer into a glass and poured a triple measure of gin. I went to add the tonic, but thought *fuck it* and drank the gin neat, grimacing as I did so. I carried the bottle and my glass back to the sitting room, set them on the small table beside my chair and continued weighing up my options, limited though they were.

My thoughts were disturbed by a knock at the door. Strange, my security app hadn't notified me of any movement. It was a calm knock, no urgency or violence. I hoped it was the police, perhaps come to question me regarding my own report to them. I again opened the app, and there was the figure, smiling up at the camera. For the first time, I had a proper look at his face. He didn't look good for his fifty-something years. His hair was patchy, mostly bald, with what little remained grey and matted. His eyes were hollow in his face, surrounded by dark craters. He offered a wave to the camera whilst smirking excitedly.

There seemed to be no point in ignoring him. I padded over to the door, gripped by both anger and trepidation. I took a deep breath and opened the door.

# CHAPTER TWENTY-NINE

## ALICE

Eight months passed, with Alice remaining on the locked ward. She wasn't the only patient on the ward but made no attempt to talk with any of the others. She had seen how easily they could become angry and violent, laughing one moment and screaming the next. Sometimes she felt like she didn't belong here, but knew that if she was to ever leave, Niel's torture could well be physical as well as mental. He would certainly hurt her as much as possible while still keeping her alive.

Alice had perfected her ability to keep her mind and spirit separate from her body. She often felt as though she were but a ghost, watching somebody else trapped in a wheelchair and a hospital ward from which she could not escape. It was the only way she could cope, the only way that Niel's incessant mocking and degrading words carried less weight and burned away at her with a little less heat. The times when her body occasionally fell asleep were worse, as Niel was free to enter her dreams, whether this was really him or her own mind playing tricks she wasn't sure, but no matter what he did to her there she couldn't force herself to wake up, the detachment from her body almost complete. During her waking hours, which numbered much more greatly than the sleeping, she suffered intermittent visual hallucinations, seeing black veins snaking from the eyes of her fellow patients.

There were only three occasions that Alice uttered any words during this eight-month period. The first was when Detective Waters visited her in the first month.

"Alice, I need to inform you of something that may not be easy to hear. We're actively looking for your former partner, Niel, in relation to a recent murder charge. Your parents have also been missing for several weeks now. Their neighbours reported them missing when they hadn't seen them in a few weeks. We found that there were flight tickets booked in their names, but they never boarded the plane. Might you have any idea as to their whereabouts?" Waters was sure there would be no response but had to ask, regardless. Alice was pulled forcefully back into her body.

"Yes," her voice cracked, and though barely a whisper, startled Waters. "Niel killed them. They're buried in the backyard. He killed them because I told my mum that I'm pregnant."

"That is a very serious allegation, Alice. Are you quite sure?" She drifted away from her body once more, and did not speak to the detective again, despite the repeated questioning. The faintest of smiles passed her lips as she hoped the police would catch Niel. She doubted that would stop the mental assault, but at least nobody else would get physically hurt if he was locked away, or so she told herself.

The second occasion came seven months later. Alice was now due any day and was undergoing a routine check-up from one of the nursing team.

"Everything looks great, Miss Hamilton. Your baby is in the correct position and should be here any day now."

"Don't let him hurt my baby." The nurse was even more shocked than Waters had been as Alice spoke. "I know he will try to hut my little boy. Please make sure to keep him away."

"Nobody is going to hurt your baby. But please let me call your social worker to come and explain a few things to you, okay?"

Within a couple of hours, Rosalia, the social worker, arrived at the hospital.

"Hello, Alice. How are you feeling today?" she asked, expecting no response, and getting none.

"We've had this conversation more than once before, and I don't think you heard a word I said, but please try to listen this time. Your ex-partner won't be able to hurt your baby. As you know, he is wanted for murder, and remains on the run from the police. And as you yourself aren't able to care for your baby, he will be placed into the care system. He will be adopted quickly. Very young babies usually are. Do you understand what I'm telling you?

"Yes," was all Alice could manage.

The next day, Alice's water broke, though the nurses weren't aware for over an hour, as Alice hadn't noticed herself. When the nurses came to force her medication on her as they did throughout the day, the alarm was raised, and Alice was rushed to the maternity ward. As the contractions started, she was suddenly present once more in her body. She felt no pain, her paralysis robbing her of what should be one of the most difficult yet rewarding physical acts the human body is capable of. Tears gently rolled from her eyes as she wept for her child's future, and she prayed, as hard as she could, for his protection from the evil she had been ruined by. A natural birth was possible due to the low position of the break in Alice's spine. She lay there, merely a bystander to the birth of her child, the encouragement of the maternity nurses meaning nothing to her.

Without even realising she had given birth, she heard a cry. For the first time in longer than she could remember, she felt a pang of love. Her emotions juxtaposed one another as she was both overwhelmed with relief and regret that her baby had been born, it had happened; she had birthed Niel's child as he had wanted. The nurse carefully carried the baby over to Alice and offered him to her, informing her that it was a boy. She was allowed to hold him briefly before he would be cared for by the hospital before being taken home by a new family.

Alice looked down at the life she had created. The life that had no idea of how it came to be and was the image of beauty and purity. She knew that she would never be allowed to care for this child, and for the first time, the thought crushed what little spirit she had left. Crying freely, she held him close to her chest and kissed the top of his head.

"Goodbye, Brandon. I'll pray for you."

# CHAPTER THIRTY

## BRANDON

He stood at the doorway smiling, and I stood to one side to let him in.

"That's it, Brandon. There's no reason why we can't be civil with one another is there."

"Ci...Civil?" I stammered. "How has any of this been civil?"

"Come on, Brandon, calm down. Let's take a seat. Have a drink. I'll have one too, while you're at it." Not knowing what else to do, I walked into the kitchen, bemused, dropped a few ice cubes into two glasses, and went back to the sitting room to find Niel looking relaxed on the sofa as though this were a social meeting. I poured two double measures of gin from the bottle on the side table, topped them up with tonic and handed one to Niel. He raised his glass as though to cheers me. I remained still.

"Sit down, Brandon." I obeyed.

"Do you know what you've done by sending your daughter away with that thing you still insist on calling your wife? That was not a smart move, Brandon. Didn't I warn you about her?"

"I'm not buying into this anymore. That's total bullshit. I looked into her eyes and I could tell that she is still my wife. She hasn't changed. There's no inexplicable thing living inside of her, controlling her. The same can't be said for you. I know all about you." I picked up the files from the orphanage and threw them at him. Niel remained unphased.

"I see. Well, that makes no difference. In fact, I'm glad you know all about me and your mother. I can finally be honest with you. I will make you kill your wife and child, Brandon. Do you know why? Because that will make sure that when you die, there's only one direction you'll be headed. All the way downstairs. Hell."

"And why do you want to send me there?"

"There's part of me in you, Brandon. The real me. It can't come out up here, but when we're reunited in Hell, I'll draw that part of me out of you. And I'll consume you. A soul of my own bloodline is a powerful thing indeed." Niel's matter-of-fact mannerisms were opposing the terrible threats he was making. I believed every word he said.

"Well, I'm glad to tell you that I'm never going to hurt Stephanie or Lily," I said defiantly, unsure where my sudden confidence came from.

"Oh Brandon, you should know better by now. I can be *terribly* persuasive." The dark veins instantly protruded from his eyes, snaking and flailing in the air. The awful black substance I had seen before oozed from his pores. Niel stood and approached me. I stood to meet him.

"You're not a man with a high pain threshold, Brandon. That's the route I'll try first. Now, I know what you're going to say. There's no pain I can inflict on you that would make you inflict pain on your family, so spare me. I'm not going to touch you. But I am going to hurt you. You've experienced my aura before. You could barely even crawl. You felt like your eardrums were about to burst. So, every single agonising sensation that you're about to experience, know that your family will be feeling exactly the same. As you lie on the ground in front of me, pathetic as you are, you'll beg me for one last chance to end their suffering."

The moment Niel finished speaking, the agonising aura returned, twice what I had felt before. I collapsed onto the ground as he had said I would. The floor beneath me vibrated and shook under the force. I felt as though I were aflame without burning, drowning without being underwater. *This is all in my head*, I told myself. All of this has always been in my head. The only power he holds over me is suggestion. He is in a human body, after all.

Thoughts of my family came to me, the perfect beauty of Lily, the purity of her innocence, her voice that causes my heart to swell when she tells me she loves me. I thought of Stephanie, my gorgeous wife, who loved me enough to put up with all of my inadequacies. And I also now believed that she had more than likely only had an affair because of Niel. He surely orchestrated that as part of his plan to corrupt me. The first step that I foolishly climbed. Suddenly, I no longer felt any pain. I could move, I could stand, and from the expression carving its way onto Niel's face, he was as shocked as I was. I felt a mental strength that I had never possessed before. I was in control for the first time in my life.

"How?" Niel asked, looking slightly afraid.

"I'm not sure." I smiled. "You did say part of the real you is in me. Perhaps I'm not as weak as you thought." Despite my bravado, I had no idea what to do next. Niel lunged at me, swinging his fists, relying on human strength instead. His first punch caught me on the side of my head, sending me reeling. I'd never been in a fight before, and certainly not one like this. I staggered back a couple of steps and avoided Niel's next swing. I threw a punch of my own, but it seemed to hardly even register with Niel as he immediately threw another of his own. I wasn't going to win this fight. And I was certain that now he knew his plan would not come to fruition. He would simply kill me instead, and then my family.

Niel stood above me, towering over my prone position on the floor, and kicked me, over and over, my ribs succumbing and breaking to his strength. My head lolled to the right, and I saw under the sofa the matches that I had dropped there and been too lazy to pick back up. I had an idea that almost certainly wouldn't work, but I tried anyway.

As Niel drew his leg back to punish me with another kick, I gathered the final reserves of my strength, grabbed his foot and twisted, sending him to the floor. I picked up the matches and stood as fast as I could with the fractures in my ribs grinding together. I staggered over to the small table, picked up the bottle of gin and hurled it, catching Niel in the chest, smashing the bottle and covering him in the flammable liquid. With trembling hands, I drew a single match out of the box, struck it once and the match caught fire. I placed it back into the box of matches, the instant blaze burning my hand. I hurled the flaming box at Niel, who immediately went up in flames, the conflagration searing his skin, cooking and melting his flesh.

Niel's screams rang through me, a sound I will never forget. He writhed on the carpet, black veins spiking out from every orifice on the body of the man who should've been my father. They slashed and drilled into the walls and the floors, slowly lengthening as they left Niel's body. His screams quietened until his body was mute, the last of the veins snaking through their new-formed burrows. The empty body burned and melted, the flames rapidly proliferating onto the sofa, the carpet. I collapsed back onto the floor, beaten, bruised and broken, but victorious. I smiled as I succumbed to the smoke rapidly filling the room, content in the knowledge that my family was safe.

# Epilogue

## Three Months Later

Stephanie had been spending a lot more time with Lily over the past three months. She had dropped her hours at work ever since the fire had burned down our home. The blaze had shown her just how fragile and precious life is, how nothing can be taken for granted, how every moment should be savoured.

The new house was smaller, of course. Money was tight now. But they had each other. Stephanie would forever be grateful that no harm had come to Lily. She had been shown the terrible things that could have happened to her, but they had not come to pass. She constantly thanked me silently under her breath.

The police that had been waiting outside the house, watching for signs of a drug deal, had kicked the door down as they saw flames flickering through the window. They were greeted by two bodies, one ablaze and obviously dead, and the other motionless on the floor, fate unknown. They called for an ambulance immediately.

I had awoken several hours later in hospital, having suffered no major injuries, the smoke inhalation and my fractured ribs being the main causes for concern. One of the nurses realised I had regained consciousness and told me that they had contacted my wife, who was on her way. It wasn't long before we were all reunited, safe, together.

Three months had passed with no sign of Niel. I allowed myself to accept that as his body burned, the evil spirit inside him had no choice but to drag itself back down to hell as it's tether to the physical world became a useless, incinerated mess of flesh and bone.

"Are you sure you're ready for this?" Stephanie asked as I put on my shoes and grabbed my car keys.

"I'm sure. I need this, and I think she does too," I said with a faint smile.

"Well, call me, okay?" Stephanie asked with concern. I kissed her, and then Lily, and headed out of the door.

The drive took about an hour and fifty minutes. I couldn't wait to get to my destination, but felt an almost overwhelming anxiety about what I would see when I got there. Butterflies beat their wings in my stomach, my fingernails tingled, and my mouth was dry. But I knew this was the right thing to do. I just prayed she would think so, too.

As my satnav told me in its robotic voice that I had reached my destination, I entered the car park and paid the fee. Not knowing exactly where I was going, I approached the front desk and asked the receptionist for direction, which she gave with a smile.

After walking for several minutes, I'd found it. I took a deep breath and spoke to the nurse at the desk.

"Hello, my name is Brandon Chapman. I've come to visit Alice Hamilton."

"Ah, of course, great to meet you Brandon," she replied. She sounded like the same nurse I'd spoken to on the phone. "Please, come this way." She led me into the ward where my mother had lived for more than thirty years. "Now, I know you're aware that your mother is non-responsive, so please, don't be too upset when she doesn't reply to you. It's not personal."

"I understand," I said, as she opened the door to Alice's room and closed it gently behind me. I looked at the woman in front of me, sat in her wheelchair. She looked older than her fifty years, her hair grey and lifeless, her skin pale and wrinkled. I sat on the chair beside her.

"Hello, Mum," I said. "It's me, Brandon."

For the first time in a very long time, Alice listened. She heard the man sitting beside her use her son's name. She turned her head and looked at him, saw him with her own eyes from inside her own body, no longer watching from above.

"That's right, it's me, Mum. Everything is okay now. I know what has happened to you, and I've taken care of it. You can finally be free of him." Alice slowly raised her hand and took hold of my own. She looked into my eyes and smiled, before closing them. A look of relief spread across her face. We sat like that for some time, hand in hand, not needing any words, content in the knowledge of each other's existence and safety.

When Alice next opened her eyes, she gasped, startling me, and stared at me with fear in her eyes.

"What's wrong?" I asked, confused.

"Black... veins..." Alice stuttered, whilst pointing a bony finger at my face. I held her closer and kissed the top of her head to calm her.

Finally, we were together again.

# About the Author

Dean Bryant is an author of thriller and horror novels, and has written various other genres under different pen names. He first got bitten by the writing bug when he was only eight years old by winning a nation-wide poetry contest.

He loves reading books from all genres, with Dean Koontz and Robert Galbraith being two of his favourite authors.

He lives in the UK with his partner of 13 years, their torti cat, Soya, and several struggling book shelves.

Dean eats a clinically inadvisable volume of spicy food, particularly Korean, Thai and Mexican. He'll also never say no to some good ol' fashioned marmite on toast.

He also works as an editor, cover designer and freelance writer.

9 781915 905499